LIMINAL PARADOX
WELCOME TO MOONVILLE
DAMON ROBI

Damon Robi Publishing
www.DamonRobi.com

ISBN 979-8-309-44133-4
First Edition: 2025
Printer in the United States of America
0 9 8 7 6 5 4 3 2 1

WELCOME TO MOONVILLE

Chapter 1
The Tunnel

I never thought I'd be one of those kids with the kind of life you see in shitty TV shows—the one who moves so much they don't bother making friends or unpacking their stuff because they know it won't be long before it's time to pack up again. That's me. Bitter as hell and done with everything.

Sixteen years old, freezing my ass off in the middle of the woods in Moonville, Ohio, because my mom thought dragging me to a ghost tour in some haunted tunnel would be "fun family bonding." Yeah, fucking right. She always pulls this local-history crap wherever we move, like learning about some dead people will make me forget we've uprooted my life for the sixth damn time.

Dad's here, too, pretending he's okay with everything as usual. He gave up a long time ago, working whatever job was available when we moved. He doesn't even argue about it anymore. He just goes along, plays the supportive husband, and does his thing. I think he's exhausted. Hell, I'm exhausted.

I blow warm air into my gloved hands and scan the small group of tourists shuffling around us like zombies. It's thirty-two degrees, and I'm standing in line to see some old, haunted-ass tunnel in the middle of the woods what a dream come true.

Ahead of me, there's a rusty bulletin board plastered with faded flyers and black-and-white photos of missing people—6 of them, dating back to 1984 and ending with one from this year. My stomach tightens as I stare at the images. Their faces look frozen in time, their smiles almost mocking. I hate shit like this. One photo catches my attention.

Stevie Whitaker, Age 15. Missing: November 27th, 2023. DOB: 12/10/2008. Her birthday was December 10th, two days before mine. Dark hair, blue eyes, and a smile that looked real—like she was the kind of person who made everyone around her feel like they belonged. She didn't belong on this damn board, none of them did. My phone buzzes in my jacket pocket, pulling me from my thoughts. It's a text from Josh.

> **Josh:** Dude, where are you? We need you on Fortnite. We're getting our asses kicked.
>
> **Me:** Can't. Stuck on some lame ghost tour with my

parents.

Josh: That sucks. Don't let any ghosts possess you or whatever the hell they do. LMAO.

Me: Na, I'm too lame to possess.

"Cove, come on," Mom says, tugging my arm. Her blonde hair peeks out from under her pink puffy jacket, giving me that look—the put-your-phone-away-or-else look.

"Jesus, Mom! You scared the shit out of me."

She glares. "Watch your language."

I roll my eyes. "How many of these dumb tours have we done? Like, 200?"

"Come on, dude," Dad says, nudging me toward the group. He's shivering, even though he swore he didn't need more than a hoodie. Mom, always prepared, brought him a beanie and gloves. Typical Dad—always underdressed and stubborn.

We join the group as the tour guide, a hunched old man with a flashlight and a voice like sandpaper, starts his speech.

"Gather around, folks. Welcome to the Moonville Tunnel ghost tour. As you can see, we've got a full moon

3

tonight. Perfect time to visit a place where tragedy and mystery collide."

My phone vibrates again, and I sneak a glance.

Josh: Anything spooky yet?

Me: Just me, dying of boredom.

Mom catches me texting and yanks the phone from my hands.

"Silent mode. Or I'm keeping it."

"Fine," I muttered, shoving the phone into my pocket.

The trees around us groan as the wind cuts through their bare branches. Fog curls around the base of the tunnel, and the bricks look like they're breathing. It's creepy as hell, but I'm not about to admit that out loud.

"The Moonville Tunnel," the guide says, shining his flashlight across the graffiti-covered walls, "has taken the lives of 25 people. The first victims were six railroad workers in the late 1800s. The train plowed through them without warning while they worked on the tracks."

The cold air stings my face, and I shift uncomfortably as the wind picks up.

"The second tragedy happened in 1984," the guide continues, lowering his voice like he's telling a ghost story around a campfire. "A teacher named Emilie Scott and 18 of her students were on a field trip when they saw someone waving a lantern in the tunnel. They thought it was a signal for help. But when they entered, the train came. None of them made it out."

Mom nudges me. "See? I told you this would be a good one."

"Yeah," I mumble, my attention drifting to the girl standing next to me. How the hell did I not notice her before? She has to be about my age, with brown-highlighted hair poking out from under her mint-colored knitted beanie and a nose that curves perfectly. She's smiling softly as she listens to the guide. Crap. She just caught me staring.

"Why do they call her the Lavender Lady?" she asks, raising her hand and giving me a quick glance.

"Excellent question," the guide says, grinning like she just made his night. "She wore a lavender dress when she died. And those who smell lavender in the tunnel often claim to see her ghost."

"You believe in this stuff?" I ask her quietly.

She shrugs, her brown eyes lighting up. "Totally. I love ghost stories."

"Same," I lie—smooth, Cove.

She giggles. "I'm Sara, by the way."

I manage a small smile. "Cove."

"Well, Cove," she says, tilting her head, "I guess we'll see if the Lavender Lady shows up."

The guide calls us to move deeper into the tunnel, and we follow. I shove my hands into my pockets, trying to ignore the chill crawling up my spine from the cold.

My phone vibrates again as I can't help to pull it from my pocket.

Josh: Did you get possessed yet?

I don't answer. The wind picks up, and I smell something faint but familiar—lavender. My breath catches up with itself as I shove my phone back into my pocket and stare down the tunnel. The glow of the full moon barely penetrates the darkness, but I can see something moving up ahead. My feet move on their own, creeping closer. My heartbeat pounds like a drum in my ears, drowning out the guide's voice. The lavender scent thickens, wrapping around me like smoke. The cold air stabs my lungs. My fingers go numb. I can't stop moving. My legs aren't listening to me.

Where the hell is everyone? The group, my parents, the guide—they're gone.

Then I see her.

A woman in a torn lavender dress stands at the tunnel's center. Her face is hidden in shadows, but I see the lantern she's holding. Its light flickers like it's about to go out.

I try to scream, but my throat locks up. My legs keep moving toward her. My brain is screaming, and everything feels very wrong! No, no, no, get the fuck out of here! Wake up, Cove. Wake up.

The tunnel breathes—in and out, in and out—like it's alive. The lantern's glow blinds me, and everything goes silent except for my ragged breathing.

Then her voice whispers through the fog, "You shouldn't have come here."

The light flares, blinding me. My knees buckle.

"Cove!" someone yells, but it's too late. The tunnel swallows me whole.

Chapter 2
Welcome to Moonville

The cold breath of the tunnel pulsed against my skin, whispering secrets I couldn't understand. The lavender scent was everywhere now—so intense it drowned out everything else. My shoes crunched over loose gravel as if the tunnel itself were pulling me deeper with each step. My mind screamed, Stop walking! Turn around! Yell for help! But my body wasn't listening.

My breath fogged up in front of me, my heartbeat pounding against my ribs like a trapped animal. Then, from somewhere ahead, a flickering light. The lantern.

The ghostly flame danced on the walls of the tunnel, casting shadows that stretched and morphed like living things. I wasn't sure if I was imagining it, but I swore I saw figures in the dark—blurry shapes shifting like they were trapped between dimensions. My breath hitched. Was this what those kids saw before the train hit them?

"Cove!" a voice called behind me, muffled by the rush of the wind. It was Sara. The girl from the tour. Her voice was distant and distorted like she was calling from underwater. "Cove! Where are you going?"

I tried to respond, but my lips wouldn't move. My legs kept moving forward like a marionette being pulled by invisible strings. Suddenly, the lantern flared brighter, so bright that I had to shield my eyes. Then it flickered out, plunging everything into complete darkness. My chest tightened as panic set in. Don't freak out. Don't freak out. I try to catch my breath as my mind races.

But the darkness pressed against me like a living thing, suffocating, relentless. I stumbled, my hand scraping against the tunnel's rough brick wall. A distant train whistle howled from deep within the tunnel, growing louder, closer. Was it real? Or was it part of the ghost story?

Then, just as I thought the whistle would consume me, a warm hand grabbed my wrist and yanked me back. My legs buckled, and I fell hard onto the cold gravel. My head spun as I blinked up at the shadowy figure leaning over me.

"Cove, are you okay? What happened?" Sara's breath came in short gasps, her wide eyes reflecting the moonlight streaming in from the tunnel entrance.

I struggled to sit up, my chest heaving, my elbows on fire and tattered from the ground. "I—I don't know. I couldn't stop walking. It was like something was pulling me."

9

Sara helped me to my feet, but her grip on my arm stayed firm, like she was afraid I'd drift off again.

"I saw you heading toward the middle of the tunnel like you were in some kind of trance. I was calling your name, but you didn't respond. What did you see?"

I swallowed hard, my throat dry. "A lantern. It was flickering, and then it went out. I couldn't move. I think I smelled lavender."

Sara's expression darkened. "The Lavender Lady." Her voice was barely above a whisper, but the fear was unmistakable.

We both turned toward the tunnel, half expecting to see her standing there in the fog. But there was nothing—just the quiet rustling of leaves and the distant groan of the wind.

"We need to get out of here," I said, grabbing her hand. "Now."

We sprinted toward the tunnel entrance, our footsteps echoing like gunshots against the brick walls. The cold air burned my lungs, but I didn't care. I just wanted to be anywhere but here. When we finally burst out into the open, the moonlight felt like salvation.

I doubled over, hands on my knees, trying to catch my breath. Sara stood beside me, her breath fogging in the air as she scanned the tree line.

"Where are your parents? The tour group?" her voice scared.

I looked around, my heart sinking. The parking lot, where the tour bus had been, was empty. No people. No bus. Just our shadows stretching long across the gravel under the full moon's glow.

"They were right here," I said, panic creeping into my voice. "They couldn't have just left."

Sara hugged herself, her breath hitching. "This is bad, Cove. Really fucking bad."

A rustling noise came from the woods in front of us. We both froze. The trees swayed, their bare branches creaking like old bones. The sound grew louder—crunching leaves, snapping twigs, something big moving toward us.

"We need to go," Sara said, her voice trembling.

"But where?" I whispered.

Before she could answer, the sound of music drifted through the air. At first, it was faint, like a radio playing far off in the distance. But it grew louder as we stood there, rooted to the spot. The unmistakable opening chords of a song I knew all too well filled the night.

"Is that... Twenty One Pilots?" Sara asked, her eyes wide with confusion.

It was. But it wasn't just any song. It was *Stressed Out*, only it wasn't the version I'd heard before. The vocals were slower and distorted, synthesized like some 80s remix that someone had recorded on an old cassette tape and left to warp over time—the eerie melody mixed with the rustling of the trees, creating a symphony of dread.

Sara grabbed my arm again. "This doesn't make any sense. That song sounds like it's from the 80s."

"I know," I said, my voice barely a whisper. "But why are we hearing it."

The music grew louder, pulsing through the trees like it had a life of its own. I felt the same tugging sensation I'd felt in the tunnel like invisible hands were trying to pull me toward the woods, and then we heard an ear-piercing scream in the distance. The sound of someone in distress, someone hurt, or worse, being hurt. I've seen enough scary movies to know that this scream was not good, definitely not good!

"What the fuck was that?" Sara said, shaking me. "We need to leave!"

I nodded, trying to block out the haunting melody. "We need to get back to the town. Maybe someone there can help us." Another terrifying shriek and growl, but this time, it was a screech of something not human, something much more significant.

Sara hesitated, glancing over her shoulder at the dark woods towards the sound. "We need to go Cove! We need to go now!"

We start running in the opposite direction of the gruesome sound that we heard, our hearts pounding, the cold air burning our lungs. "The music! Run to the music!" Sara doesn't say anything, listens and continues to run until the music grows faintly louder and louder. We reach a paved road and feel safe under the glowing street lights.

In the distance, the faint glow of a large worn sign that reads *Welcome To Moonville.* The streetlights flickered through the fog like a lighthouse guiding us back to shore. But as we walked down the eerie street, I couldn't shake the feeling that we weren't walking toward safety—we were walking deeper into a nightmare. The same song plays in the distance but gets louder with every footstep we take on the asphalt.

"I think we are trapped here." Sara's voice shakes.

"What do you mean?"

"I don't know how to explain it; it's just a feeling," she said, her voice cracking as we entered the town of Moonville.

The weight of her words settled over me like a heavy fog. Was she right? Were we really trapped here? "Then what do we do?" I asked, desperation creeping into my voice.

She took a deep breath, her gaze locking onto mine. "We have to figure out what's going on; maybe we follow that music, which could lead us to whoever is playing it."

I nodded, even though every fiber of my being was screaming at me to panic. "Okay. But, first rule: Don't split up."

Sara smiled weakly. "Deal."

The sound of the music faded, replaced by the distant whistle of a train. We both turned toward the sound, dread settling in my stomach like a lead weight.

"Let's go," I said, grabbing her hand again. We took off down the wet, black paved road, the shadows of the trees stretching long and ominous around us.

The fog pressed in around us as we made our way deeper into Moonville's empty streets. The cracked sidewalks were littered with fallen leaves as old neon signs buzzed faintly, advertising diners and arcades that looked like they hadn't changed in decades. But there was no sense of nostalgia here—only decay.

"I don't get it," I muttered, shoving my hands into my jacket pockets. "This place is like stuck in the 80s, but it feels... dead and alive at the same time."

"Cove, I think we are stuck," Sara said softly, her eyes scanning the dimly lit windows around us. "And I think they're trapped. This isn't just some retro tourist town."

"Trapped?" I echoed.

Sara nodded. "My uncle told me about places like this once. Dimensions that break off from reality, where the rules of time don't work the same. This whole town is locked in an 80s version of itself, but it's not just stuck in the past—it's evolved. Look at that." She pointed to a nearby billboard plastered with an ad for a new Madonna album.

"Madonna hasn't released anything since—" I stopped. "Whoa, whoa, wait! Are you telling me this place is generating new 80s music from artists that aren't even around anymore? Do you have any idea how fucking nuts that sounds?" I can't believe what I'm hearing she fucking nuts.

Sara nodded grimly. "Not just music. Movies, TV shows, everything. It's like this dimension is feeding off the 80s and creating its own version of it. But the people here... I think some of them know they're trapped and too scared to fight it, or they don't know how to leave, maybe?" She points out movie and music posters that don't make sense.

We passed a small café where a group of teenagers sat around a table, laughing and sipping milkshakes. Their clothes were classic 80s—bright windbreakers, ripped jeans, high-top sneakers. A DeLorean was parked outside, its metallic sheen catching the dim light of the street lamps.

"They look... normal-ish, but what the fuck are they wearing?" I'm starting to think Sara might be right.

"They do," Sara agreed, "but something tells me they're not."

We turned a corner and nearly bumped into a stack of cardboard boxes piled against the side of an abandoned electronics store. The faded sign above the entrance read *Benny's Boom Box*. The windows were cracked, and inside, rows of old cassette tapes lined the dusty shelves of shop windows.

"Do you hear that?" Sara asked, tilting her head.

A faint hum of music drifted through the air—something eerie, familiar, and wrong. It was a slow, warped version of *Stressed Out* by Twenty One Pilots, but the vocals were muffled like they'd been recorded underwater.

"This is what we heard to lead us here." She softly spoke as we followed the sound to the alley behind the store. That's when we saw a small, rusted cassette tape boom box sitting on the ground next to a box of weathered tapes. The player's buttons were caked in dirt, and the tape inside spun on its own as if an invisible hand had pressed play.

"This is creepy," I said, taking a step back.

Sara bent down and carefully picked up the boom box. "It's still working, somehow." Then the music screeched to a stop, making Sara freak and scaring her enough to drop the radio, which shatters on the concrete, leaving the cassette tape alone in the black plastic pile of rubble.

My eyes instantly fell on the tape sitting there, its label taunting me it was faded and peeling, but I could make out the words scrawled in thick black ink: DO NOT PLAY.

My pulse quickened. "Hey, look."

She followed my gaze, her face paling when she read the label. "That's... not exactly a good sign."

"No kidding." I reached for the tape, but when my fingers touched it, I felt a jolt of static electricity shoot up my arm. I dropped the tape, my heart pounding. "What the hell was that?"

Sara picked it up carefully, turning it over in her hands. "It's warm."

"That's not normal," I said, wiping my sweaty palms on my jeans. "Do you think someone left this here on purpose?"

Sara frowned. "It's like it was waiting for us."
Silence filled the alley, thick and suffocating. Then, the sound of shuffling footsteps echoed from the entrance to the alley.

We spun around.

An old man stood in the shadows, his hunched figure illuminated by the dim glow of a flickering streetlamp. He wore a tattered leather jacket, and his eyes, bloodshot and sunken, seemed to pierce right through me.

"You shouldn't have picked that up," he rasped, his voice like gravel and soaked in beer. "That tape isn't for you."

I stepped in front of Sara, instinctively shielding her. "Who are you?"

"That doesn't matter," he said, his lips curling into a humorless smile. "And you're standing in the wrong place at the wrong time."

Sara tightened her grip on the cassette tape. "What's the deal with this tape? Why does it say not to play it?"

The beer-soaked man sighed, shaking his head. "Because once you play it, you'll hear things you don't want to hear. Voices from the past. People who didn't make it out of this town."

I swallowed hard. "What do you mean, didn't make it out?"

He took a step closer, his eyes narrowing. "This place doesn't let you leave. Once you're here, you're stuck. The tape is just a reminder of that. It records what the town wants you to know—what it wants you to fear."

"That doesn't make sense," I said, my head spinning. "What's on the tape? What happens if we play it?"

The man's expression darkened. "If you play that tape, you won't be able to stop it. It'll keep playing in your head, even when you take it out. And eventually, it'll lead you to her."

"The Lavender Lady," Sara whispered.

He nodded. "That bitch is the reason none of us can leave. She feeds on fear; the tape's her favorite way of finding it."

I felt my stomach twist into knots. "So, what are we supposed to do?"

"Stay away from the woods after dark," He grunted, his voice low and serious. "That's where she's strongest. And whatever you do, Do. Not. Press. Play!" He gives a horrible phlegmy cough.

I exchanged a look with Sara. I could tell she was just as freaked out as I was, but there was something else in her eyes—a spark of curiosity. This guy must have noticed it, too.

20

"Don't let your curiosity get the better of you, kid. Trust me, nothing good ever comes from messing with a tape like that." He coughs again, and without another word, he turns and disappears into the shadows of the alley, his footsteps and cough dragging into the distance.

Sara and I stood there for a moment, the weight of his warning and booze settling over us like a heavy fog. The cassette tape in her hand felt like a ticking time bomb.

"What do we do now?" I asked.

Sara hesitated, then slipped the tape into her jacket pocket. "We don't play it."

But the way her fingers lingered over the pocket told me it wouldn't be that simple.

Chapter 3
The Monster in the Woods

The town grew quieter as the night deepened, the wind whispering through the trees like secrets we weren't meant to hear. Sara and I walked down the main road toward the outskirts of Moonville, the old streetlights casting long shadows across the cracked pavement. The cassette tape sat like dead weight in her pocket, and neither of us had spoken much since we left the alley behind Benny's Boom Box.

I finally broke the silence. "You're thinking about playing it, aren't you?"

Sara gave me a sideways glance. "We have to, Cove. There's no way we'll figure out what's happening here unless we do."

I shoved my hands into my pockets and stared at the ground as we walked. She wasn't wrong. As much as I hated the idea, the tape seemed like the only clue we had. But that didn't mean I wasn't terrified of what might happen when we hit play.

"Let's at least figure out what we're up against first," I said. "That old man knew things. I bet others in town do, too."

As if on cue, a group of teens emerged from the shadows near the town's run-down bowling alley. There were four of them—two guys and two girls—all wearing 80s-inspired clothes that looked too clean to be thrift-store finds. One of the guys had a jean jacket covered in pins from old bands like The Clash and Van Halen, and the girl beside him was chewing gum loudly, blowing bubbles, and popping them like she had all the time in the world.

They spotted us and exchanged glances before the guy in the jean jacket stepped forward, his hands stuffed into his pockets. "You two new here?"

I nodded cautiously. "Yeah."

"You don't look like you're from here." His gaze shifted to Sara, then back to me. "What's your deal?"

"We're just... trying to figure things out," Sara said.

"We got stuck here after the ghost tour at the tunnel."

The guy's face darkened. "The tunnel. Figures."

"Why?" I asked, my pulse quickening. "What happens at the tunnel?"

"It's one of the ways in," he said. "But there's no way out." He snapped back.

The girl with the gum blew another bubble and popped it with a loud snap. "Unless you're not planning to stick around, you better join the rest of us and learn the rules."

"Rules?" Sara asked.

The guy in the jean jacket gestured for us to follow him. "Come on. We'll explain."

We followed them down a side street until we reached an old gas station with broken windows and graffiti covering the walls. Inside, the air smelled like mildew and motor oil, but at least it was warmer than outside. The teens gathered around a makeshift table made from an old tire and a wooden board, and the guy in the jean jacket leaned against the wall, crossing his arms.

"First rule," he said, "don't go into the woods after dark."

I exchanged a glance with Sara. "We've heard that one already."

"Yeah, well, there's a reason everyone says it," the guy replied. "The monster in the woods only comes out at night, and it's fast. If you hear the trees rustling, you're already too late."

Sara swallowed hard. "Has anyone ever survived it?"

The guy's jaw tightened. "Not many. The ones who do usually have scars to show for it."

The girl with the gum pulled out a cigarette and lit it, exhaling a cloud of smoke. "Second rule: Don't mess with the cassette tapes. They're cursed."

Sara shifted uncomfortably. "What happens if you do?"

"Depends on the tape," the girl said, blowing smoke out the side of her mouth and then continuing to chew her gum. "Some of them just mess with your head—make you see things that aren't there. Others..." She trailed off, her gaze drifting to the floor.

"Others do what?" I pressed.

The guy in the jean jacket leaned forward, his expression serious. "They don't just make you see things. They make things happen. And once they start, there's no stopping them."

I felt a chill crawl down my spine. "Then why are there so many tapes lying around town?"

"Because the town wants them here," the guy said. "It's like bait. The tapes draw people in, and once they play them, they're stuck."

"Like us," Sara said softly.

25

The guy nodded. "Exactly."

There was a long silence before Sara spoke again. "Is there any way out?"

The guy hesitated, then shook his head. "Not that we know of. Some people think the Lavender Lady knows how to leave, but good luck getting her to tell you. She's the reason this place exists."

"Why?" I asked.

"Legend says she died in the tunnel when the train hit her," the girl with the gum said. "But instead of moving on, her spirit got tangled up in some kind of curse. Now she haunts the town, feeding off fear and keeping everyone trapped."

Sara pulled the cassette tape out of her pocket and set it on the table. The guy in the jean jacket's eyes widened. "Shit! Where did you get that?"

"Behind Benny's Boom Box," she said. "Why? Do you know this tape?"

He nodded slowly. "That's one of the fucking worst ones. No matter what you do, you can't break it. If you try to smash it, burn it, whatever—it'll always come back."

I felt like the room was spinning. "So what the hell do we do?"

"Don't play it," he said firmly. "Hide it, bury it, throw it in the damn lake—just don't let it get inside your head."

But even as he said it, I could see the doubt in his eyes. He didn't believe we could avoid it any more than we did.

Sara stood up, her jaw set. "We need to find a way out, and I think the woods are our best bet. If we can get past the monster, maybe there's something out there that'll help us."

The guy in the jean jacket shook his head. "You're crazy. The woods are suicide day or night! There's always something trying to kill you out there, trying to make you afraid, so you turn around and stay."

"Then you stay here," Sara said, slipping the tape back into her pocket. "But we're going."

Another girl, who had been sitting quietly on the edge of the table, suddenly stood. Her long, dark hair caught the dim light as she walked toward us. "Wait!" I tensed, recognizing her from the missing child's poster at the ghost tour. "You're—"

"Stevie." She said, cutting me off. Her blue eyes flicked to the cassette tape. "I'll go with you."

"Why would you do that?" I asked, my stomach knotting with suspicion.

27

"Because," Stevie said, "I've been here long enough to know that hiding won't save you. I've tried it. I'm done waiting around for something to change."

Sara nodded, and without another word, Stevie grabbed a flashlight from the pile of junk in the corner. "Let's go before we change our minds."

We made our way toward the woods, the cold night air clinging to my skin like something alive. Stevie led the way, her flashlight cutting through the fog, but even she seemed tense now. The wind hissed through the trees like it was trying to warn us to turn back, and every snap of a branch beneath my boots sent a jolt of adrenaline through my body.

I opened my mouth to say something, but Stevie held up her hand. "Do you hear that?"

We froze, listening.

At first, there was only the wind. Then, faint and distant, a scream. It was sharp, cutting through the night like a knife, just like the scream we heard earlier.

"What the fuck was that?" Sara asked.

Stevie's face went pale. "Someone's out there."

The scream came again, followed by a voice—low, cold, and commanding and more of a loud growl.

Stevie's grip on the flashlight tightened. "We need to keep moving."

We broke into a run, the forest blurring around us as the fog thickened. The screams faded behind us, but their echo lingered in my head like the forest wasn't ready to let us forget.

As we sprinted deeper, a shadow leaped from the fog. I barely had time to react before I was tackled to the ground.

I screamed, flailing my arms as I tried to fight off whoever—or whatever—had hit me. My flashlight rolled away, its beam casting wild shadows on the trees.

"Relax! It's just us," the guy in the jean jacket said, grinning down at me.

I blinked up at him, my heart racing. "What the fuck is wrong with you?"

The rest of the teens emerged from the fog, their flashlights casting eerie beams of light. "We figured you'd need backup," the girl with the gum said, popping another bubble.

Stevie scowled. "This isn't a game."

"I know," the guy said. "But you'll be glad we're here when you see what's out there."

29

I wasn't sure if I trusted them, but we didn't have much of a choice. Stay here and exist or die trying to get home.

We started moving again, deeper into the woods. The air thickened with the scent of lavender, suffocating and cloying. Somewhere ahead, something growled low and guttural, sending chills down my spine.

"We're close," Stevie whispered. "And it knows we're coming."

Chapter 4
Secrets of the Cassette Tape

The air clung to me like a wet blanket as we trudged deeper into the woods, the fog swirling around our legs. Stevie led the way, her flashlight steady, but her shoulders tense, like she expected something—or someone—to jump out at any second. The scent of lavender was still faint, but it was there, clinging to the back of my throat like poison.

"We can't keep stopping," Stevie said, glancing over her shoulder at Sara and me. "The longer we're out here, the more dangerous it gets."

Sara clutched the cassette tape tightly in her hand, her knuckles white. "We need to listen to it," she said. "If we don't, we'll be running blind."

"I know," Stevie said, her jaw clenched. "But we're not listening to it out here. We'll find a better spot."

We walked in tense silence for another few minutes until we reached a small clearing surrounded by thick trees. The fog wasn't as heavy here, and the ground was dry enough to sit without soaking our clothes. Stevie gestured for us to sit.

Sara pulled the cassette tape out of her pocket, staring at the faded DO NOT PLAY label as if it might change its mind and say something more practical, like Classic Rock Mix or anything other than DO NOT PLAY, and then in fine print, hey BTW I'm a cursed tape and will kill you. "Does anyone have a player?"

The guy in the jean jacket smirked and shrugged off his backpack. "You're in luck." He unzipped the front pocket and pulled out a portable cassette player—one of those bulky, clunky models with headphones already attached, the kind with orange foam earpieces.

"Of course, you have one," Stevie muttered under her breath.

The bubble-gum girl blew another bubble and popped it with a loud snap. "What? He's the type?"

"Yeah, yeah," the guy said, rolling his eyes. "But let's be clear. Whoever listens to this thing is taking a risk."

"I'll do it," Sara said immediately, but I grabbed her arm.

"No way," I said. "You've already done enough. Let me."

"You don't even want to be here," she argued, her voice rising slightly. "If anyone's going to listen to the creepy death tape, it should be me."

"The whole fucking town doesn't want to be here!" I snap back.

Stevie stepped between us. "Both of you need to calm the fuck down. This isn't a competition to see who's braver. We need to be smart about this."

The guy in the jean jacket tossed the cassette player onto the ground between us. "Someone pick. We're wasting time."

Everyone went silent, the tension so thick I could hear the sound of my own pulse. I stared at the cassette player, the dull plastic reflecting the glow of the flashlights. My mouth felt dry, but I forced the words out. "I'll do it."
Sara started to argue, but I cut her off. "I said I'll do it."

Stevie handed me the tape. "You sure about this?"

No, I'm not sure, but nod my head. "Yeah."

I took the cassette and slid it into the player, my hands shaking slightly as I pressed it into place. The headphones felt heavy as I placed them over my ears, the padded orange cushions muffling the sounds of the forest. My thumb

33

hovered over the PLAY button momentarily before I forced myself and pressed down.

Static hissed through the headphones, crackling like an old radio trying to find a signal. I adjusted the volume, wincing as the static grew louder. Then, beneath the noise, I heard it—a faint voice distorted and distant.

"Help me."

The words sent a shiver down my spine. I turned the volume up and leaned forward, straining to hear more.

"She's coming. Run."

I ripped the headphones off and tossed them onto the ground, my breath coming in short, panicked gasps. "The voices—they're from the people who've gone missing I think. They're warning us."

Sara picked up the headphones and pressed them against her ear, listening for a moment before nodding. "They're begging for help."

Stevie swore under her breath. "That means it's already started. The tape isn't just a recording—it's a fucking signal."

"To who?" the guy in the jean jacket asked.

"To her," Stevie said grimly. "The Lavender Lady."

The bubble-gum girl popped another bubble and laughed nervously. "You guys are acting like this is a horror movie."

"It is," I muttered.

Before anyone could respond, the air around us shifted. The wind picked up, rustling the trees, and the scent of lavender intensified, choking the air. I covered my mouth and nose, but it didn't help. My eyes watered, and I could barely breathe.

"Something's wrong," Stevie said, her voice sharp. "We need to move—now!"

The bubble-gum girl didn't listen. She stood there, chewing her gum and grinning. "Relax. There's nothing out here."

Then, without warning, something exploded out of the fog behind her. A shadowy figure with long, twisted limbs and glowing eyes. My brain barely had time to register what I was seeing before it grabbed her by the waist, yanked her onto the floor, and then dragged her into the trees. She screamed horrifically, her bubblegum-pink nails clawing at the ground as she tried to hold on to anything. Her nails scour to grip something as all of her pink nails tear off, and blood fills all of her fingertips.

"Help! Help me!" Her voice screams trailing off into the distance.

We rushed forward, but it was too late. The shadow dragged her into the darkness, her screams cutting through the night like knives. I saw a glimpse of her wide, terrified eyes before she disappeared completely. Then her ripped-apart torso was flung at our feet from the darkness, her lifeless face staring at us with blood-filled eyes, her intestines seeping from under her torn ringer t-shirt.

"Fuck!" The guy in the jean jacket yelled, stumbling back.

Stevie grabbed my arm, her nails digging into my skin. "We can't help her."

"We can't just leave her!" Sara cried, tears streaming down her face.

"She's gone," Stevie said firmly, her voice cracking. "If we don't move, we'll be next."

I stared into the trees, my mind racing. The girl's screams had finally stopped replaying in my head, but the sound of something chewing echoed faintly through the fog. My stomach turned as I could hear the cracking of her bones.

Stevie yanked me backward. "Cove! Let's go!"

36

I forced my legs to move, following Stevie and the others as we ran through the woods. My heart pounded against my ribs, and my breath came in ragged gasps. The cassette player bounced against my leg as I ran, the cursed tape still inside. Another blood-curdling scream and the other boy that came with them disappeared with a yank from his head, his body then being flung and smashed on a tree, his bones cracking louder than the limbs of the tree. His head was then thrown at us like a bowling ball trying to knock us down, blood splattering us all with every roll.

We didn't stop running until we reached another clearing, our flashlights flickering like dying stars.

"What the fuck was that?" the guy in the jean jacket asked, doubling over and gasping for air.

"The monster," Stevie said, her voice hollow. "And it's not done."

The fog thickened around us, and I knew she was right. We weren't safe. Not even close.

Chapter 5
A Dangerous Deal

We sat huddled in a shallow cave near the edge of the woods, the jagged rock walls pressing against our backs as the fog crept closer. My legs trembled, and every breath felt like I was sucking in knives. Sara sat beside me, her head buried in her hands as she sobbed quietly, her hands splattered with blood. Stevie kept watch near the entrance, her flashlight off to avoid drawing attention. The cassette player sat between us like a cursed artifact, its tape still spinning silently.

"I think it's gone," Stevie whispered, her voice cracking.

"We just let her die." The lump in Sara's throat barely let her talk.

I didn't know what to say. The image of a helpless girl being dragged into the woods was burned into my brain. I never even got her name; I never knew if she was trapped here like us or if she was born in this hell. Her screams echoed in my ears, and I felt like I could still smell the faint sweetness of her gum mixed with the lavender-scented fog.

"She wasn't your fault," Stevie said softly, her gaze focused on the trees. "If we had stayed, we'd be dead too."

"She deserved better than that," Sara said.

"We all do," Stevie replied, her voice hollow.

The guy in the jean jacket sat cross-legged on the ground, staring at the cassette player. "This fucking thing is going to get us all killed."

"It's not the tape," Stevie said, turning toward him. "It's the town. The tape is just one of the ways it fucks with you."

I leaned back against the rock wall, my head spinning. "So what do we do now?"

"We wait," Stevie said. "If we move now, we'll be sitting ducks."

The wind howled through the trees, and I could hear the distant sound of something—or someone—moving through the fog. My fingers twitched, and I clenched them into fists to stop the shaking. Then, the mist shifted. It wasn't natural, the way it moved. It swirled and danced, forming shapes that didn't belong. A figure emerged from the mist, gliding silently across the forest floor. My heart stopped when I saw her.

"It's her," I say softly. She was beautiful in the most unsettling way, her pale skin glowing faintly in the moonlight. Her long black hair cascaded over her

39

shoulders, and her dress—a tattered, ghostly thing—billowed around her like it had a life of its own. Her eyes, deep and dark, locked onto mine.

"Cove," she said, her voice like a lullaby. "Come here."

I felt the pull immediately like invisible strings were wrapped around my body, dragging me toward her. My legs twitched, and I fought to stay where I was, but it was like trying to resist gravity.

"Cove!" Stevie grabbed my arm, shaking me. "Don't listen to her!"

The Lavender Lady smiled, a soft, knowing smile. "I can help you," she said. "I can show you the way out."

Sara scrambled to her feet, standing between me and the ghostly figure. "Leave him alone!"

The Lavender Lady's gaze shifted to Sara, her smile fading slightly. "You don't understand what you're dealing with, child. I'm the only one who can help you."

"Bullshit," Stevie said, pulling me back against the wall. "You've been keeping people trapped here for decades."

The Lavender Lady tilted her head, her dark hair falling across her face. "And you think you can change that without me?"

"What do you want?" I asked, my voice barely a whisper.

Her gaze returned to me, and she smiled again. "A deal."

My throat went dry. "What kind of deal?"

"Find the truth," she said, her voice soft and melodic. "Uncover the secrets of this town—the secrets that caused the curse in the first place. If you do, I'll let you leave."

"That's it?" Sara asked, her voice dripping with skepticism. "No strings attached?"

The Lavender Lady's eyes gleamed. "There are always strings, my dear."

"We're not fucking stupid," Stevie said. "You wouldn't be offering us a way out unless you needed something."

The Lavender Lady sighed, her gaze flicking toward the fog. "The curse binds me here as much as it binds you. If you break it, we're both free."

"And if we fail?" I asked.

Her smile widened, and a shiver ran down my spine. "Then you'll become part of this place, just like the others."

I swallowed hard, my mind racing. "How do we start?"

"You already have," she said, nodding toward the cassette player. "The answers are hidden in the voices of those who came before you. Follow their trail. Find the truth."

Stevie's grip on my arm tightened. "We can't trust her."

"We don't have a choice," Sara said, her voice barely above a whisper.

The Lavender Lady began to fade, her body dissolving into the fog like smoke. "Good luck, Cove. You'll need it."

When she was gone, the forest fell silent. The fog swirled around us, but the suffocating scent of lavender had faded slightly.

"What the fuck just happened?" the guy in the jean jacket asked, his voice shaky.

"We made a deal with a ghost," I said.

"And now," Stevie added, "we have to make sure we don't end up like her last victims."

Chapter 6
Facing the Monster

The forest was eerily quiet as we made our way down the narrow dirt path, the fog swirling around our legs like it was trying to pull us back. My flashlight flickered, casting shaky beams of light across the twisted trees. I adjusted the batteries, praying it wouldn't die at the worst possible moment.

"Do you hear that?" Stevie asked, her voice barely above a whisper.

I strained my ears, but there was nothing—no wind, no rustling leaves, no distant animals. Just silence. The kind of silence that pressed against your ears and made your skin crawl.

"We shouldn't be out here," the guy in the jean jacket muttered, kicking at a root. "We should've stayed in the cave."

I rolled my eyes and adjusted the strap on my backpack. "You've been complaining the whole time. What's your name, anyway?"

He hesitated for a second as if unsure whether to answer. "Riley."

"Nice to meet you, Riley," I said sarcastically. "You gonna keep whining, or are you actually gonna help?"

"Fuck off, man," Riley shot back, but there was no bite behind his words. "I'm just saying we're walking right into its territory."

Stevie shot him a glare. "If we stay in one place, we're as good as dead. We have to keep moving."

"We're getting closer," Sara said, her breath fogging in the cold night air. "I can feel it."

"Feel what?" I asked, even though I already knew the answer.

"The monster," she replied. "It's watching us."

The hair on the back of my neck stood up. I scanned the trees, my flashlight shaking slightly in my hand. The shadows shifted as the beam flicked across the underbrush, but nothing moved. At least, not yet.

"Let's just keep going," Stevie said, motioning for us to follow her. "If we're lucky, we'll find a place to set up a perimeter before it gets too close."

"Lucky," Riley muttered under his breath. "Yeah, sure."

We moved silently for a few more minutes, the only sounds from our boots crunching on dead leaves and the occasional snap of a twig underfoot. My mind was racing, replaying the Lavender Lady's words over and over again. Find the truth. Follow their trail.

"What if the monster isn't just guarding the town?" I said suddenly, breaking the silence.

Stevie glanced back at me, her brow furrowed. "What do you mean?"

"I mean, what if it's connected to the curse?" I looked around at the fog-covered woods. "What if it's not just some random creature but part of whatever's keeping us here?"

"Great," Riley said, throwing his hands in the air. "So now we're fighting a supernatural guard dog."

"Not fighting," Stevie corrected him. "Surviving."

Just as she said that, the fog shifted ahead of us, swirling unnaturally before parting like a curtain. My breath caught in my throat as a shadowy figure emerged from the mist. At first, it was hard to make out—just a tall, dark shape moving slowly through the trees. But as it drew closer, the details became horrifyingly clear.

The monster was massive, its body covered in thick, matted fur that seemed to shimmer in the moonlight. Its eyes glowed a sickly yellow, and its limbs were long and twisted, with claws that dragged against the ground as it

45

moved. It didn't walk so much as glide, its feet barely touching the earth.

"Holy shit!" Riley whispered, taking a step back.

"Don't run," Stevie warned, her voice steady but low. "If you run, it'll chase you."

The monster stopped about twenty feet away, its glowing eyes locked on us. My chest felt like it was being crushed under the weight of its gaze. It let out a low, guttural growl that vibrated through the ground, making the leaves tremble.

"What do we do?" Sara asked, her voice barely audible.

Stevie didn't answer right away. She stared at the monster, her fingers gripping the flashlight so tightly that her knuckles were white. "We need to distract it. If we can lure it away, we might have time to find what we're looking for."

"Lure it away with what?" Riley asked, panic creeping into his voice. "We don't exactly have bait."

Stevie's gaze shifted to the cassette player dangling from my backpack. "We do now."

My stomach dropped. "You want me to play the tape?"

"It's already connected to the Lavender Lady," she said. "If we play it, maybe it'll confuse the monster long enough for us to escape."

"Or it'll piss it off," Riley said.

"We don't have a choice," Stevie snapped. "Cove, do it."

My hands trembled as I reached for the cassette player. I fumbled with the buttons, my fingers slick with sweat, and slid the tape inside. My thumb hovered over the PLAY button, and I took a deep breath.

"Here goes nothing," I whispered, pressing PLAY and cranking up the volume. The static crackled to life, loud and grating, cutting through the silence of the forest like a chainsaw. The monster flinched, its head snapping toward the sound. For a moment, it just stood there, listening. Then, the distorted voices began.

"Help me. She's coming. Don't let her—"

The monster roared, a deafening sound that shook the trees and sent a flock of birds scattering into the sky. Its eyes glowed brighter, and it lunged forward, its claws tearing into the ground as it closed the distance between us but then darted into the other direction into the woods, its howls of pain echoing in the night.

47

"Run!" Stevie shouted.

We took off, sprinting through the woods as fast as our legs could carry us as I shoved the player in my back pocket to avoid losing it. The trees blurred past me, and the sound of the monster crashing through the underbrush was like thunder in my ears. My lungs burned, and my legs felt like they were going to give out, but I didn't stop. Then, the cassette player clicked. The tape was finished, and the player automatically rewound itself, the soft mechanical whirl filling the air. My blood turned to ice.

"Oh, fuck," Riley said, glancing over his shoulder. "It's coming back."

I yanked the cassette player out of my backpack, my fingers fumbling with the buttons as I tried to stop the rewind. The monster's footsteps grew louder, crashing through the trees like an oncoming train.

"Cove!" Stevie screamed.

"I'm trying!" I yelled, slamming my thumb on the PLAY button just as the monster burst through the fog, its glowing eyes locked on me. The static blared from the bright orange headphone speakers again, and the monster skidded to a halt, its claws digging into the dirt. It let out another deafening roar before retreating into the shadows.

48

My heart pounded in my chest as I collapsed to the ground, gasping for breath. "We can't stop the tape," I said between gulps of air. "If it's not playing, it can track us."

"We'll run out of tape eventually," Sara said, trembling. "What happens when we do?"

I didn't have an answer.

"We keep moving," Stevie said, pulling me to my feet. "And we hope to God we find the next clue before this thing catches up to us."

With the cassette player still blaring static, we stumbled through the fog, the monster's roar echoing in the distance. We didn't have much time.

Chapter 7
Breaking the Curse

The fog felt thicker as we made our way deeper into the woods, suffocating and clinging to my skin. My legs burned, and my lungs strained for air, but I couldn't stop. Not with the monster prowling somewhere behind us, lurking just out of sight.

"We're getting nowhere," Riley said, panting. "We've been running for what? An hour? We need a fucking plan."

"We're trying to figure it out," Stevie shot back. "Unless you know exactly how to lift a decades-old curse, I'd shut the fuck up if I were you!"

"Guys," Sara interrupted, her voice shaking, "We're wasting time arguing. Cove, what do you think?"

I slowed down, my brain scrambling for anything—any clue we'd missed. My thoughts drifted back to the ghost tour and the stories the guide had told us. He'd said something important about the Lavender Lady that we hadn't paid enough attention to. My breath hitched as the memory hit me:

The following incident occurred in 1984, where a teacher, Emilie Scott, who many know as the Lavender

Lady and 18 elementary school children were out for a mid-day walk field trip. They saw someone swinging a lit lantern in the tunnel and calling for help, and then, with no warning, the train came again, killing all 18 children, including the Lavender lady."

"She was a teacher," I said suddenly, stopping in my tracks. "The Lavender Lady, Emilie Scott, was an elementary school teacher in the 80s. The tour guide mentioned it."

Stevie frowned. "So?"

"Maybe we're looking in the wrong place," I said, heart pounding. "If she was a teacher, maybe there's something at the elementary school. Old records, papers, anything that could help us piece this together."

Stevie's eyes widened with understanding. "You think she left something behind?"

"She had to," I said. "The curse started with her death. The key to breaking it might be tied to whatever she was trying to tell people before the accident."

Riley groaned. "Of course. Breaking into a haunted elementary school in the middle of the night while a monster and a psychotic ghost are after us. Fantastic!"

"Let's move," Stevie said, ignoring him. "We don't have much time."

The abandoned Moonville Elementary School stood in eerie silence, its cracked brick walls covered in ivy and its windows shattered like broken glass eyes. The wind rattled through the hollow building, and the front doors sagged on their hinges as we pushed them open.

Our footsteps echoed inside the empty hallway, the tile floors chipped and stained. Dust coated everything—desks, lockers, even the faded posters that still clung to the walls, their colors long since drained by time.

"This place is a graveyard," Riley muttered.

Stevie's flashlight swept across the hallway. "We need the main office. School records should be in there."

We found the office door half-open, the room beyond cluttered with old filing cabinets and stacks of yellowed papers. Stevie rummaged through the drawers while Sara and I flipped through the files on the desk. The air smelled of mildew and decaying paper, making it hard to breathe.

"Got something," Stevie said, pulling out a folder. She opened it to reveal the faculty roster for 1984. "Emilie Scott, first grade. Room 104."

"That's our next stop," I said, stuffing the folder into my backpack.

We crept down the hallway, passing empty classrooms with dust-covered desks and abandoned textbooks scattered across the floor. When we reached Room 104, the door creaked as I pushed it open, revealing rows of tiny desks arranged neatly in lines. The walls were covered in children's drawings, their faded crayon marks barely visible.

Stevie made a beeline for the teacher's desk, opening drawers and rifling through old lesson plans, attendance sheets, and then a bottle of perfume, which Stevie sprayed without hesitation.

"It's lavender! Guys, this has to be her desk! This must be why she's called the Lavender Lady." She resprays it for others to smell. The mix of the sweet flowers with the mildew-covered walls makes an eerie smell of death. Continuing to search through the messy desk, and finally, at the bottom of the largest drawer, she found it—a small, leather-bound diary with "E.S." embossed on the cover.

"This has to be hers," she whispered, holding it up.

But before we could open it, the cassette player crackled to life, filling the room with static. My heart jumped as ghostly voices echoed from the speakers of the headphones, growing louder and more frantic through the headphones.

"You shouldn't be here. She's coming." The voices murmured.

Sara covered her mouth, her eyes wide with fear. "It's the kids."

The static intensified, and the voices became a chorus of desperate whispers.

"Get out. Run The curse is waking up."

I spun toward the window just in time to see the fog shift outside. Heavy footsteps echoed through the hall, and a familiar, guttural growl rumbled through the building.

"The monster," Riley whispered, backing away from the door.

Then, the static stopped. The cassette player whined and clicked off. My blood went cold.

"The batteries," Stevie said, her voice barely above a whisper. "It's dead."

Before anyone could react, the classroom door exploded inward, splinters flying as the monster barreled through. Its glowing yellow eyes locked onto us, letting out a deafening roar, shaking the walls.

"Move!" Stevie yelled.

We sprinted out of the classroom, the monster's thundering footsteps behind us. My flashlight bounced wildly in my hand as we tore down the hallway, dodging debris and broken lockers. The scent of lavender choked the air, making it hard to breathe.

"Where the fuck are we going?" Riley shouted.

"We need batteries!" Stevie yelled back. "There's gotta be some in the supply closet."

We veered down another hallway and skidded to a stop in front of a door marked "Supplies." Stevie yanked it open, and we stumbled inside, slamming the door shut behind us.

The monster roared outside, clawing at the walls.

"Find the batteries!" Stevie shouted, frantically digging through boxes of old school supplies. Sara and I tore through the shelves, tossing aside markers, notebooks, and broken calculators.

"Here!" Sara cried, holding up a pack of AA batteries. My hands shook as I ripped open the package and loaded the batteries into the cassette player.

The monster slammed against the door, cracking the wood.

"Any day now!" Riley yelled.

I hit PLAY, and the static blared to life, followed by the Lavender Lady's voice.

"I'm sorry. I'm so sorry. Please let them go." An eerie female but controlling voice echoed.

The monster let out a final, ear-splitting roar before its glowing eyes flickered and dimmed. Its massive body convulsed, then dissolved into the fog, leaving nothing behind but claw marks on the floor.

The room fell silent, except for the Lavender Lady's voice still playing softly through the speakers, repeating the same sentence until it became static again, with the faint song of *I wear my sunglass at night* by The Valiant Thieves.

I opened the diary and flipped through the pages, skimming the shaky, frantic handwriting. Emilie Scott had been consumed by guilt, but it wasn't the guilt I expected. It wasn't an accident at all.

October 30th, 1984—*The voices won't stop. The children cry out to me even when I'm at home. They say I failed them, that they'll never be free unless I free them myself.*

November 2nd, 1984—*Today, I saw a train schedule. The timing is perfect. I've planned a field trip to the tracks.*

We'll all be there when the train passes through. No one will suffer anymore. The children will be free, and so will I.

November 5th, 1984—*I don't want to do this, but they won't leave me alone. They say they're trapped, and they're right. They'll be trapped forever unless I end it.*

My throat tightened as I read the last entry:

November 16th, 1984—*I have the lantern. I'll swing it when the train comes just like the voices said. They promised it would all stop once we joined them on the train. I'll be with them when it's over.*

I closed the diary, my hands trembling. She had orchestrated the entire thing—the deaths of her students, her death—because she thought it was the only way to free them from whatever haunted them. Instead, she had trapped them in Moonville's nightmare.

I locked eyes with Stevie. "She caused the curse."

"And now," Stevie whispered, "we have to fix it."

"Don't tell me back to the tunnel?" Riley complained.

"Yup, back to the tunnel." I reluctantly repeat.

Chapter 8
The Final Showdown?

The wind howled as we raced through the woods, the glowing entrance of the Moonville Tunnel visible in the distance like a haunting beacon. My legs ached, and every breath felt like I inhaled glass shards, but I didn't stop.

The diary entries kept repeating in my head. Emilie Scott had believed she was saving her students, but instead, she'd condemned them—and herself—to an endless nightmare. Now, we had one chance to end it.

"Faster!" Stevie shouted, her voice barely audible over the wind. "We have to beat it there!"

Behind us, the monster's guttural growl echoed through the trees, closer than I wanted it to be.

"We're not gonna make it!" Riley yelled, panting. "It's too fast!"

"We have to!" Sara cried, clutching the cassette player to her chest. "Just keep running!"

The monster crashed through the underbrush, its glowing yellow eyes cutting through the fog like headlights. I could hear its claws scraping against the ground, tearing through roots and branches as it gained on us. The scent of lavender was overpowering now, thick and suffocating.

"We're almost there!" Stevie said, pointing ahead. The tunnel loomed just beyond the tree line, its archway glowing faintly in the moonlight.

But then, without warning, Stevie screamed.

I skidded to a stop and turned around, my heart dropping into my stomach. Stevie had fallen to the ground, her leg sinking into a large puddle of water that glistened unnaturally under the moonlight.

"Help!" she cried, struggling to pull herself free. "I can't get out!"

I rushed to her side, dropping to my knees. "What the hell is this?"

The puddle wasn't just water—it was alive. The surface rippled like liquid glass, and tendrils of black, inky fluid coiled around Stevie's leg, pulling her deeper. Her foot had already disappeared, and the water was up to her calf.

"Cove!" she screamed, clawing at the ground, dirt and blood filling under her nails. "It's dragging me under!"

Sara and Riley skidded to a stop beside us, their eyes wide with panic.

"Grab her arms!" I yelled. "We have to pull her out!"

Riley grabbed her left arm, and I took her right. Sara crouched beside us, frantically trying to loosen the tendrils wrapped around Stevie's leg.

The monster's growl grew louder, and I risked a glance over my shoulder. It was closing in fast, its glowing eyes locked on us.

"Shit," Riley muttered, pulling with all his strength. "We don't have time for this!"

"I'm not leaving her!" I shouted, digging my heels into the ground as I pulled.

The water rippled violently, and then more tendrils wrapped around Stevie's other leg. She screamed, tears streaming down her face as she kicked and thrashed.

"Let me go!" she sobbed. "It's gonna take me under!"

"Shut up!" Riley snapped, his voice shaking. "We're not letting you die!"

Sara tore at the tendrils with her hands, ripping them apart one by one, but they kept reforming, latching onto Stevie's legs and waist like barbed wire. I could feel the muscles in my arms burning, but I didn't let go.

"We need something sharp!" Sara cried. "We have to cut her free!"

"There's nothing!" Riley shouted, his face red with exertion.

The monster roared, and I turned just in time to see it burst through the trees, its massive body illuminated by the moonlight. Its claws tore through the ground as it lunged toward us, its glowing eyes filled with rage.

The cassette player in Sara's hands blared static, but it wasn't enough to keep the monster at bay. We needed more time. Desperation clawed at my chest as I yanked harder, my fingers digging into Stevie's wrist.

"I'm not letting you die!" I growled, pulling with everything I had.

Stevie's leg popped free of the water with a final, bone-jarring tug, and we all tumbled backward, landing in a heap on the muddy ground. The tendrils hissed and recoiled, sinking back into the puddle. She screams as pain surges from her leg. The monster didn't let go; it was her skin that gave way and peeled off her leg. We all looked at her in agony.

"Go!" Stevie gasped, her chest heaving. "We have to go!"

But as we scrambled to our feet, disaster struck. In the chaos, Sara had accidentally knocked the cassette player against a rock, and the STOP button had been pressed. The static cut off abruptly, leaving only the sound of the monster's heavy breathing.

"Oh shit," Sara whispered, her eyes wide with terror. "I stopped the tape."

The monster's eyes flared brighter, letting out a deafening roar that shook the trees. Its claws tore through the ground as it lunged toward us, faster and more ferocious than before.

"Play it! PLAY IT!" Riley screamed.

Sara's hands shook as she fumbled with the buttons, desperately trying to press PLAY. But the monster was already upon us, its massive form blocking out the moonlight as it reared back, ready to strike.

I grabbed a large branch from the ground and swung it with all my strength, hitting the monster across its face. The impact barely fazed it, but it bought Sara a few precious seconds.

She hit PLAY, and the static blared to life just as the monster's claws grazed my shoulder, gashing my arm with three deep claw marks. I stumbled backward, pain shooting down my arm and blood dripping to my fingertips, but the monster recoiled, its glowing eyes flickering as the Lavender Lady's voice filled the air.

"I'm sorry. I'm so sorry. Please let them go."

The monster thrashed wildly, its body convulsing as the voice echoed through the forest. I grabbed Stevie's hand and pulled her to her feet, my shoulder screaming in protest.

"We have to get to the tunnel!" I yelled, gripping the cassette player as tightly as I could. "Now!"

We sprinted through the trees, the monster's pained howls fading behind us. The tunnel was just ahead, its archway glowing with an eerie, silvery light. My legs burned, and my breath came in ragged gasps, but I didn't stop.

As we reached the entrance, I turned around and saw the monster collapsing to the ground, its body dissolving into the fog-like smoke. But I knew it wasn't gone for good. Not yet.

"We have to end this," Stevie said, clutching my arm. "We're so close."

I nodded, gripping the cassette player like it was a lifeline. The Lavender Lady's voice still played softly through the static, her final confession on an endless loop.

"Let's do this," I whispered, stepping into the tunnel's cold embrace.

Chapter 9
Escape from Moonville

The tunnel's cold breath wrapped around us, damp and reeking of mildew and something metallic—like rusted metal soaked in blood. The dim light at the other end flickered weakly, as though it were struggling to stay alive. Our footsteps echoed off the curved brick walls, mixing with the distant hum of the Lavender Lady's voice still playing through the cassette player.

"I'm sorry. I'm so sorry. Please let them go."

Stevie limped beside me, her face pale and drawn, as Sara helped her forward. Riley kept close behind, his flashlight flickering in and out. My own breathing came in heavy gasps, every muscle in my body ached, and my shoulder was on fire, but I didn't dare slow down. The scent of lavender was overpowering now, filling my nose and mouth, as though the air itself was trying to choke me.

"Something's wrong," Sara said, glancing at the dimming light ahead. "The tunnel—it doesn't feel right."

I felt it, too. The bricks seemed to pulse, like the tunnel itself was alive, breathing in time with our footsteps. The light flickered again, dimming further.

"We just have to make it to the end," I said, my voice hoarse. "We're almost there."

But as we pressed forward, the static on the cassette player shifted. The Lavender Lady's voice, once mournful and broken, grew sharper. More controlled.

"Don't go."

My stomach twisted. "Did she just—?"

"Come back", her voice purred through the speaker, soft but commanding. "You belong here."

Sara's hand trembled as she gripped the player. "She's not apologizing anymore."

"No," Stevie whispered, panic flickering across her face. "She's trying to stop us."

The light at the tunnel's exit blinked completely, plunging us into darkness.

"Run!" I shouted, yanking Stevie forward as Sara and Riley followed. The tunnel's walls seemed to close around us, and the scent of lavender thickened, clinging to our clothes and skin. My flashlight flickered wildly, casting erratic beams of light that only made the shadows seem more alive.

Then, from the darkness behind us, the familiar guttural growl echoed—low and menacing.

"She's here," Riley choked out, his voice cracking. "The monster."

"No," Stevie gasped. "It's her. The Lavender Lady and the monster—they're the same."

Before I could fully process her words, the growl grew louder, accompanied by the wet slap of claws on the tunnel floor. I risked a glance over my shoulder, and my blood turned to ice.

Her human form was gone. In its place, the monstrous creature we had been running from all night charged after us—its glowing yellow eyes burning like twin suns, its massive, fur-covered body rippling as it moved. But now, I saw the truth. The faint outline of her human face flickered beneath the monstrous façade, her eyes weeping ghostly tears that mixed with her rage.

"She's been using the tapes," I realized, my voice barely audible. "Her voice. It's part of the trap."

"Cove, focus!" Sara yelled, yanking me forward as the monster's claws scraped against the brick walls, sending sparks flying. "We have to make it to the end!"

The cassette player blared another line, but this time her voice wasn't begging.

"You'll never leave me. None of you will."

The ground beneath us trembled like the tunnel was reacting to her anger. Chunks of brick crumbled from the walls, and the air was thick with dust and lavender. My legs burned as I sprinted, dragging Stevie with me. The light ahead flickered back to life, but it was weak, barely illuminating the end of the tunnel.

"We're not going to make it," Riley gasped, stumbling over a loose brick.

"Yes, we will," I growled, refusing to let fear take over.

The monster roared behind us, and I could feel her breath on the back of my neck, hot and rancid. My mind raced, searching for a plan, anything that could buy us more time. Then I remembered—the cassette player.

"Sara, the tape!" I yelled. "Turn it off!"

"What?!" she shouted, panicked.

"Just do it!"

She fumbled with the buttons, her fingers shaking, and the tape stopped abruptly. The silence followed was deafening, broken only by the monster's growl. For a split second, it hesitated as if confused by the sudden absence of its own voice.

"Now, play it again!" I screamed.

Sara hit PLAY, and the Lavender Lady's voice crackled back to life, distorted and furious.

"You can't escape me."

The monster convulsed, its massive body shaking as the human form of the Lavender Lady flickered in and out of existence. Her ghostly face twisted in pain, her mouth opening in a silent scream.

"Keep moving!" Stevie cried, limping toward the light. "It's working!"

We reached the tunnel's exit just as the monster lunged, its claws swiping through the air inches from my back. I stumbled onto the grass, the cold night air hitting me like a slap. Stevie collapsed beside me, gasping for breath, while Sara and Riley tumbled to the ground.

The monster stopped at the tunnel's edge, its glowing eyes locked on us. It just stood there for a moment, its body flickering between its monstrous form and the ghostly image of the Lavender Lady. Then, slowly, it retreated into the tunnel, disappearing into the darkness.

The cassette player clicked as the tape reached its end.

We sat in stunned silence, the only sound the distant rustling of leaves and the wind whistling through the trees.

My hands shook as I turned to look at the tunnel, half-expecting the monster to reappear.

"Did we do it?" Riley asked, his voice barely above a whisper.

"No," Stevie said, wiping blood from her lip. "Not yet."

I followed her gaze to the cassette player. The tape was still intact, and its final message was waiting to be heard. The Lavender Lady wasn't gone. Not completely.

"We have to destroy it," I said, my voice steady despite the fear clawing at my chest. "For good this time."

Stevie nodded. "But not here. She's still too strong."

"We'll find the right place," Sara said, standing and helping Stevie to her feet. "We'll end this once and for all."

As we stumbled away from the tunnel, I felt the weight of the cursed town pressing down on me. The fight wasn't over, but for the first time, I believed we had a chance.

Behind us, the tunnel glowed faintly, the scent of lavender lingering in the air like a warning.

Chapter 10
Back to Reality?

The grass beneath my feet felt real. The cool breeze brushing against my face was real. But as I stood at the edge of the woods, staring at the familiar gravel road that led back to town, a gnawing feeling in my gut told me something was wrong.

Stevie leaned against a tree, her breathing shallow as she tried to ignore the stabbing throbbing pain in her leg, but tears still rolled down her cheeks as the adrenaline wore off. Sara stood beside her, gripping the cassette player as though it would disappear if she let go. Riley paced back and forth, kicking rocks with every step.

"Do you feel that?" Sara asked, her voice barely a whisper.

I nodded, swallowing hard. "It's too quiet."

Even the crickets, which had been chirping incessantly when we entered the woods earlier, were now silent. The trees stood like sentinels, watching us with their gnarled branches. The path that should have led us back to the highway stretched endlessly, disappearing into the horizon.

"We made it out of the tunnel," Riley said, his voice strained. "We should be home by now."

"We're not," Stevie whispered. "We're still trapped, look!" She stands by the Missing Children's board, shining her flashlight at her portrait, but then reveals mine and Sara's portraits.

"What the fuck, how long have we been gone?" As I walked forward, the gravel crunched beneath my shoes, my flashlight casting a weak beam over the endless dirt path. My heart pounded in my chest, and my fingers felt numb as I gripped the straps of my backpack and stared at the tunnel.

Sara walked beside me, her gaze fixed on the cassette player, tears running down her cheeks. She hadn't let go of it since we'd left the tunnel, and I couldn't blame her. It felt like our only lifeline, even though it had brought nothing but pain and terror.

"I don't get it," Riley said, kicking another rock into the trees. "We did everything right. We faced the monster. We have the tape. Why are we still here?"

"It's the curse," Stevie said, leaning heavily on Sara for support. "It's not going to let us go that easily."

My throat tightened. "What if we can never leave?"

Sara shook her head violently. "No. We're getting out of here. We just need to figure out what the next step is."

We walked in silence for a few minutes, the trees whispering around us as the wind picked up. The scent of lavender had faded, but it still lingered faintly, like a ghost we couldn't shake.

Then, up ahead, something glinted in the moonlight. Wait," I said, holding out my arm to stop the others. "Do you see that?"

Stevie squinted, her flashlight sweeping across the road. "It's something on the ground."

We approached cautiously, our footsteps slow and deliberate. My stomach churned as I realized what it was— a cassette tape. It lay there in the middle of the road, its black plastic casing gleaming like it had just been dropped.

"No," Sara whispered, her voice cracking. "No, no, no. Two of these goddamn tapes!"

I knelt down, picking up the tape. My hands shook as I read the label written in neat, blocky letters: PLAY ME.

Riley backed away, shaking his head. "Nope. Fuck that. We're not doing this again."

"We don't have a choice," Stevie said grimly. "It's part of the curse. We'll be stuck here forever if we don't play it."

"But what if playing it just makes things worse?" Sara asked, tears streaming down her face. "What if this is how it starts all over again?"

I turned the tape over in my hands, its weight pressing down on me like a physical force. We had fought so hard and lost so much. And now, the curse was dangling one final carrot in front of us, daring us to take the bait.

"I don't know," I admitted. "But if we don't try, we'll never know."

I placed the tape into the cassette player with sticky, blooded, trembling fingers and, without hesitation, hit PLAY.

The static crackled to life, loud and grating. I braced myself for the Lavender Lady's voice, but instead, there was silence. Just the sound of the tape whirring as it played.

Then, a new voice emerged faintly—soft, broken, and unmistakably familiar over the headphones.

"Cove."

My breath caught in my throat. "What the hell?"

"Cove", the voice repeated, louder this time. It wasn't the Lavender Lady. It was me—my own voice, distorted and hollow, coming through the speakers.

The others stared at me, their eyes wide with confusion and fear.

"What is this?" Sara asked, grabbing the player, her voice barely audible.

I didn't have an answer. The tape continued to play, my voice overlapping with itself in a chaotic jumble of words and phrases I didn't recognize.

"You never left. The curse isn't broken. She's still here." My voice scratches through the silence and the tape as it echoes deeper.

Suddenly, the tape screeched, and the Lavender Lady's voice cut through the noise, sharp and cruel.

"Did you really think it would be that easy?"

The air around us grew colder, and the ground trembled beneath our feet. I ripped the cassette player out of Sara's hands and slammed it against the ground, but it didn't stop. The tape kept playing, the sound reverberating through the trees.

"You belong to me now, the Lavender Lady whispered. Just like they did."

Behind us, the tunnel glowed again, brighter this time. The scent of lavender returned, stronger than ever. My pulse raced as I turned around and saw her standing at the tunnel's entrance—her human form flickering, barely holding together as the monstrous shape of the beast threatened to take over.

"We have to run," I said, grabbing Sara's hand.

"Where?" Riley shouted. "There's nowhere to go!"

The trees around us twisted and warped, their branches reaching out like skeletal hands. The dirt path seemed to stretch endlessly in both directions, like a cruel illusion.

"Cove," Stevie said, her voice trembling. "We can't run forever."

I knew she was right. The curse wasn't something we could outrun. It was inside us now, part of us.

"We have to destroy the tapes," I said, my mind racing. "Completely this time."

"How?" Sara asked. "We tried everything. It's unbreakable."

"Fire," Stevie said, her eyes narrowing. "We have to burn it. The tunnel is where the curse started—maybe if we destroy it there, it'll be enough."

I didn't wait for anyone to argue. I grabbed the tapes and sprinted toward the tunnel, my heart pounding like a drum in my chest. The others followed close behind, their footsteps thundering against the ground.

The Lavender Lady watched us from the entrance, her face a mixture of fury and sorrow. Her ghostly form flickered violently, and for a moment, I thought I saw the faces of the children she had taken, their eyes hollow and pleading.

"Don't let them suffer anymore," I whispered.

We reached the tunnel, and I threw the tapes onto the ground. Stevie pulled a lighter from her pocket and flicked it on, her bloodied hands shaking. The tiny flame danced in the wind as she knelt and held it to the tape.

For a moment, nothing happened. Then, the plastic casing melted, and the tape inside caught fire. The flames roared to life, crackling and spitting as they consumed the cursed object. The Lavender Lady let out a blood-curdling scream, her form twisting and contorting. The ground shook violently, and the tunnel's walls cracked, chunks of brick falling around us.

"Get back!" Riley yelled, pulling Stevie to her feet.

We stumbled out of the tunnel just as the flames engulfed the last of the tapes in a ghostly flame. The Lavender Lady's screams faded, and the glow of the tunnel dimmed until it was nothing but darkness.

Silence fell over the woods.

"Did it work?" Sara asked, her voice barely above a whisper.

I didn't answer. I couldn't. My mind was racing, my heart still pounding. Slowly, I turned around and saw the path behind us. The trees were still. The air was clean. And for the first time, the scent of lavender was gone.

"We're free," Stevie said, her voice filled with disbelief.

I wanted to believe her. I really did. But as we walked back toward the road, I couldn't shake the feeling that something was still watching us.

And when I saw another cassette tape lying in the dirt, its label reads: PLAY ME, my heart sank instantly.

Chapter 11
The Road

The gravel crunched beneath our shoes as we walked forward, my flashlight casting a weak beam over the endless dirt path. My heart pounded in my chest, and my fingers felt numb as I gripped the strap of my backpack. Every step felt heavier like the weight of the town itself was pressing down on us.

Sara walked beside me, her gaze fixed on the cassette tape in her hands. She hadn't let go of it since we found it lying in the dirt, the label mocking us with its simple message: PLAY ME.

"We shouldn't have taken it," Riley muttered, kicking a loose rock into the trees. "We burned the last two. We should've just left this one behind."

"We didn't have a choice," Stevie replied, her voice strained. "It's part of the curse. Ignoring it won't make it go away."

Sara's grip tightened around the tape. "What if this one's worse?"

I looked at her, my throat tightening. "It doesn't matter. We have to know what it says."

The wind whistled through the trees, and the scent of lavender, faint but persistent, tickled the edges of my senses. Even when it wasn't overpowering, it was there, like a reminder that the Lavender Lady was always watching.

We walked in silence for a few more minutes, the path stretching endlessly ahead of us, its gravel surface crunching in the same monotonous rhythm. My pulse quickened as I realized we'd passed the same broken branch twice. We were going in circles.

"I told you," Riley said, stopping abruptly. "We're trapped. The road's looping back on itself."

My heart sank. "No. There has to be a way out."

Stevie collapsed onto the side of the path, wincing as she adjusted her leg. "Cove, it's not working. We've been walking for hours."

I rubbed my hands over my face, trying to think. If the curse wasn't going to let us leave, then we had missed something—something the Lavender Lady wanted us to find.

My gaze fell on the tape in Sara's hands. My stomach churned. "We need to play it."

"What?" Sara said, her voice trembling. "Cove, we don't know what's on it."

"That's the point," I said. "We won't figure out what's keeping us here until we know what she's trying to tell us."

Riley groaned. "Or it'll just summon the monster again, and we'll die."

"Then we better hope it doesn't," I said, taking the tape from Sara's hands and loading it into the half-busted cassette player. My fingers trembled as I pressed PLAY, leaving a sticky, bloody fingerprint behind.

The static crackled to life, making me flinch. I thought the tape was broken for a second, but then, faint and distorted, a familiar synth melody bled through the static.

"Oh, fuck," Sara whispered. "Is that—?"

I recognized it too. *Blinding Lights* by The Weekend— but it wasn't the version we knew. Just like the other songs from our time, the synths were warped, dragging out each note like something from an 80's horror film. The beat slowed down, the lyrics twisted into an echoing, haunting loop:

"I said, ooh, I'm blinded by the lights..."
"No, I can't sleep until I feel your touch..."

The distorted melody played for several seconds, the synths growing louder until they became a wailing hum that made my ears ache.

Then, just as suddenly, the song cut out, replaced by the Lavender Lady's voice.

"You thought you could leave, she whispered, her voice laced with bitterness. Moonville isn't done with you yet. You've burned two tapes. There are more. And one of them holds the key to your freedom. Maybe."

The static hummed for a moment, and then the haunting chorus of *Blinding Lights* faded back in, this time more warped and dissonant. The lyrics slurred together like the song itself was falling apart:

"I said ooooooooh..."
"I'm blinded by the lights..."

Suddenly, the Lavender Lady's voice cut off, and a new voice bled through the static—deep, male, and panicked.

"This is Stationmaster Henry Black," the voice said, his words rushed and clipped. "To whoever finds this, listen carefully. The cargo we were transporting wasn't supposed to be on the tracks. I warned them. I told them the route wasn't safe, that Tunnel 5 wasn't..."

There was a brief pause, followed by the sound of labored breathing.

"I had no choice. They forced the detour. They said the train had to pass through the tunnel, no matter what. But something was waiting for it there."

Sara gasped, her hands flying to her mouth. "What does he mean?"

I gritted my teeth, listening as Henry Black continued.

"I saw it—something moving alongside the train. It wasn't human. It wasn't anything I'd ever seen before."

The tape crackled again, and Henry Black's voice lowered to a whisper.

"If you're hearing this, you're already in danger. Find the cargo manifest. It's the only way you'll understand what's really happening here. And whatever you do, don't let it find you first."

The tape clicked, and the distorted melody of *Blinding Lights* returned, warping and fading until it cut off completely.

We sat in stunned silence, the weight of Henry Black's words pressing down on us like a suffocating blanket.

"The cargo?" Stevie whispered, her voice barely audible. "It wasn't just ordinary freight."

"It's connected to the curse," I said, my mind racing. "Whatever was on that train triggered everything. That's why the Lavender Lady haunts the tunnel. It wasn't just the train accident—it was what the train was carrying."

Riley groaned, rubbing his face. "So, what now? We go digging through an abandoned train station looking for records from forty years ago?"

"Yes," I said, standing and pulling my backpack onto my shoulders. "That's exactly what we do. Do you know the way?"

"I fucking hate you! Fuck! Follow me it's not fucking far," he mumbles and throws a tantrum. "I wish I had Doc's goddamned DeLorean so I can erase you guys from my existence."

We all looked at each other, smiled at his rant, and let Riley lead the way. It was the first time any of us had cracked a smile in a while, which was soon gone after we reached the edge of where the train station began.

The station looked like it had been swallowed by time. Ivy and vines crawled over its crumbling stone walls, and the windows were cracked or completely shattered. The rusted tracks that once ran through the platform were barely visible beneath the weeds and debris.

"We don't have much time," Stevie said, glancing over her shoulder. "The Lavender Lady knows we're here."

We climbed over the rusted turnstile and made our way to the main building. The scent of mildew hit me the moment we stepped inside, mingling with the faint, ever-present smell of lavender. Broken benches and torn posters littered the floor, and the walls were covered in graffiti, some of which looked fresh.

"There's gotta be an office or something," I said, shining my flashlight toward a hallway where my light spotted a sign marked STAFF ONLY.

We moved cautiously, the floor creaking beneath our feet. The hallway was narrow, lined with doors that led to long-abandoned offices and storage rooms. At the end of the hall, we found a door labeled STATIONMASTER.

Stevie tried the handle. It was locked.

"Step aside," Riley said, pulling out a metal rod he'd picked up outside. With a few sharp jabs, the lock gave way, and the door swung open.

"Hey, look, Riley, you're good for something!" Stevie smacked his shoulder as she passed him to go inside.

"Yeah, well, don't forget I'm also your fucking tour guide, apparently, in this hell hole!" He shoots her a glare as he drops the metal rod which echoes down the halls.

Inside, the air was thick with dust, and the shelves were lined with faded books and files. A large wooden desk sat in the center of the room, its surface covered in papers that had yellowed with age.

Sara went straight to the desk, rifling through the stacks of documents. I checked the filing cabinets, pulling out folders and flipping through them as fast as I could.

"Here," Sara said, holding up a train schedule from 1984. Her fingers trembled as she pointed to the bottom of the page.

There, in bold letters, was the same note from the tape: **Emergency detour approved under special circumstances. Authorization granted by Stationmaster Henry Black**.

"But what was the cargo?" Stevie asked, scanning the papers.

Before anyone could answer, the faint sound of static filled the room.

"No," Stevie whispered, backing away. "Not again."

The cassette player blared to life, screeching *Highway to Hell*, by AC/DC until then, Lavender Lady's voice cut through like a knife.

"You shouldn't have come here."

The lights flickered, and the air grew icy. My breath fogged in front of me as the floor trembled beneath our feet. Then, from the shadows in the corner of the room, a pair of glowing yellow eyes appeared.

"She's here," Riley whispered, his voice barely audible.

The monster emerged from the darkness, its massive form blocking the hall where we entered. Its claws scraped against the floor, sending sparks flying as AC/DC burst through the headphones.

"*Highway to Hell!*"

"Run!" I yelled, grabbing Sara's hand.

Chapter 12
The Tunnel Reopens

We sprinted down the hall, thinking we can find a way out, our footsteps thundering against the floor as the monster roared behind us. My flashlight bounced wildly, casting shadows that made everything look like it was shifting and alive. The scent of lavender grew stronger, thick enough to make my throat burn, and the monster closed in behind us.

Riley yanked open a door marked SUPPLY ROOM and gestured for us to get inside. "In here! Now!"

We bolted through the doorway, slamming the door shut just as the monster's claws raked across the metal door. The door groaned, but it held. For now.

Stevie collapsed against a shelf filled with rusted cans of oil and old tools, her breath coming in ragged gasps. Sara slid down the wall, clutching the cassette player to her chest as if it were a lifeline.

"That thing's not fucking giving up," Riley said, leaning against the door to reinforce it.

"It's because we're close," I said, my mind racing. "She doesn't want us to find out what the train was carrying."

Sara wiped the sweat from her brow and nodded. "Henry Black said the cargo manifest would explain everything. Maybe it's around here somewhere."

I shone my flashlight across the room. The supply room was cluttered, with rusted equipment, stacks of forgotten boxes, and shelves sagging under the weight of old ledgers. Dust hung in the air, thick and suffocating.

"We'll split up," I said, swallowing my panic. "Look through everything. The manifest has to be here."

I rifled through a stack of yellowed papers on a nearby shelf, my fingers trembling as I flipped through them. Most of it was junk—maintenance logs, employee schedules, and outdated inspection reports.

Riley was digging through a pile of boxes in the corner, tossing old tools and broken radios aside. Stevie sat on the floor, flipping through a binder with frayed edges, her injured leg stretched out in front of her. The monstrous Lavender Lady stopped clawing at the door which made me nervous. I felt like she could pop out of somewhere that we weren't seeing that had an opening.

Sara searched the far wall, where a filing cabinet leaned against a stack of crates. She tugged on the drawer, but it wouldn't budge. "Cove, help me with this."

I rushed over and grabbed the handle. Together, we pulled, and with a screech of metal, the drawer finally slid open. Papers spilled out, scattering across the floor.

"There!" Sara pointed to a large envelope with MANIFEST – NOVEMBER 1984 stamped across the front.

I grabbed it, tore it open, and pulled out the sheets inside. My heart pounded as I scanned the pages. The first few listed routine cargo—coal, timber, steel beams. But then, at the bottom of the page, a handwritten note caught my eye.

CARGO ITEM #237: SPECIAL HANDLING REQUIRED. CLASSIFIED. DO NOT OPEN WITHOUT CLEARANCE.

"What the hell is special handling?" Riley asked, peering over my shoulder.

"It doesn't say," I muttered, flipping through the other pages. "There's nothing here about what it actually was."

Stevie frowned. "Maybe it wasn't just one thing. Maybe it was multiple things."

I turned the last page and found another note, scribbled hastily in the margin:

Checkpoint interference reported. Unidentified object attached to cargo. Proceed with caution through Tunnel 5.

"What the fuck does that mean?" Sara whispered, her voice trembling.

"Something was on the train that wasn't supposed to be there," I said. "And it followed them into the tunnel."

Stevie's eyes widened. "And it's been here ever since."

The room trembled, and the sound of splintering wood from the door jams echoed through the walls. The monster started trying again as if she was quiet to hear us talking. She's trying to break down the door, its growls vibrating the floor beneath us.

"We need to get out of here," Riley said, grabbing the manifest. "The longer we stay, the worse this will get."

I nodded. "There has to be another way out. Train stations like this usually have maintenance tunnels, right?"

Sara's face paled. "You want us to go underground?"

"It's either that or wait here to die," I said. "Which do you prefer?"

"How the hell do we get past psycho killer mutated werewolf ghost bitch?" Riley screams as the pounding on the door gets louder.

I look around the room, and there's nothing, no windows or other doors. Then, I look up. "The ceiling!" I whisper loudly.

"Come on, man!" Riley complains.

"It's our only way the ceiling tiles probably connect to another room." I look around the room at everyone.

"Who the fuck cares at this point." Sara whispers loudly, "Boost me up. I'll go first."

I cup my hands, ready for her foot, as she gets the hint and doesn't hesitate. She flies upward with ease as her other foot goes on my shoulder. She slides a ceiling tile over and lays flat inside the ceiling.

"Come on!" She says quietly.

Riley comes and tries to go next, and I glare at him, "Lady's first!"

"Fine!" He whispers and shoots me an aggravated look. I squat slightly again for Stevie, cup my hands, and toss her up.

"Now you!" I get into stance as Riley doesn't hesitate, pushing him right up with a grunt from his weight. The pounding and scrapping won't stop on the door; the metal and wood framing holding for now.

"Cove! Come on!" Sara looks down at me, worried.

"Go! I'll be right there!" I grab a broken office chair with only three wheels left and drag it to the opening. As the pounding stops, I stand on the wobbly chair and hear loud sniffing around the door's cracks. I can't help but think she knows exactly what we are doing and will find us in the ceiling, peeling the ceiling tiles back like we are sardines in a tin can. I give myself one good thrust with my already soar legs and grab the frame of the ceiling, where Riley helps me up.

"The girls found a way out." He whispers as a loud shrieking cry from the monster rattles the tiles around us, and then we hear her running down the hall.

We finally left the supply room, down the cobwebbed ceiling, and into a janitorial closet where the girls were waiting for us. We peeked cautiously out the door and moved quickly down the hall, the flickering beams of our flashlights guiding us through the maze of corridors. The scent of lavender was everywhere now, choking and heavy, and my skin crawled with the feeling that we were being watched.

"There." Stevie pointed to a steel door with a sign that read MAINTENANCE ACCESS. I yanked it open, revealing a narrow staircase leading downward into the dark.

Riley shone his flashlight down the steps. "This just keeps getting better."

"Come on," I said, leading the way down. The stairs groaned under our weight, and the air grew colder the farther we descended. At the bottom, we found ourselves in a long, narrow tunnel lined with pipes and cables.

The walls were damp, and water dripped from the ceiling, forming shallow puddles on the floor. The faint sound of machinery hummed in the distance like the station was still alive even though it had been abandoned for years.

"Which way?" Sara asked, her voice echoing off the walls.

I checked the map on the wall, tracing my finger along the routes. "This tunnel leads directly to Tunnel 5. If the cargo interference happened there, we'll find something."

We moved cautiously, our footsteps splashing through the puddles. The further we went, the darker it became, as if the light from our flashlights couldn't penetrate the shadows. My pulse quickened, and I kept glancing over my shoulder, half-expecting the monster to burst through the wall.

Then, up ahead, I saw it—a rusted metal door with TUNNEL 5 ACCESS stenciled across it.

"We're here," I said, my voice shaking. I grabbed the handle and pulled. The door groaned but didn't budge.

"Move," Riley said, shoving past me. He kicked the door hard, and it flew open with a deafening clang.

The scent of lavender hit me like a punch to the gut, and I staggered backward, coughing.

"What is this place?" Stevie whispered.

The room beyond the door was massive, with high ceilings and rows of abandoned equipment. The train tracks ran through the center of the room, disappearing into the darkness on either side. Rusted freight cars sat on the tracks, their sides covered in graffiti.

But it wasn't the trains that caught my attention. It was the pile of crates in the corner, their wooden sides splintered and broken as if something had clawed its way out.

One crate was still intact, its lid nailed shut. I approached it cautiously, my heart pounding in my ears.

"Cove," Sara said, her voice trembling. "Don't."

But I had to know. I pried the lid open and shone my flashlight inside when a rat jumped from the opening and scared me. "Fucking shit!"

"What the hell!" Riley shines his light on me.

"Stupid damn mouse," I reply and shine my flashlight back into the opening. At first, I thought the crate was empty. But then I saw something small and metallic, glowing faintly in the beam of my flashlight.

I reached in and pulled it out.

It was a cassette tape.

The label was smeared and faded, but I could make out the words written in black ink: FINALE MESSAGE.

The room trembled, and the walls groaned.

"She's coming," Stevie said, backing away. "We need to leave. Now!"

I stuffed the tape into my backpack and turned toward the exit. But before we could move, the monster's roar echoed through the tunnel, louder than ever.

"RUN!" I shouted.

Chapter 13
What Lies Beneath

We sprinted through the maintenance tunnel, our footsteps splashing through puddles of stagnant water that seemed to stick to the bottom of our shoes. My breath burned in my lungs, and the weight of my backpack pressed down on my shoulders like a boulder, but I didn't dare slow down. The monster's growls echoed behind us, reverberating through the walls like the roar of an oncoming train.

Riley was ahead of us, his flashlight bouncing wildly as he navigated the twists and turns of the tunnel. Stevie hobbled beside me, her injured leg slowing her down, but she didn't complain. Sara kept pace on my other side, clutching the cassette player to her chest.

The scent of lavender grew stronger with each step, clinging to my clothes and invading my lungs. My mind raced, replaying Henry Black's warning: The cargo wasn't supposed to be here. And now, it's waiting for you.

"We need to find a place to hide," Stevie gasped, clutching her side.

"There's nowhere to hide," Riley called over his shoulder. "We have to keep moving."

A loud splash behind us made my blood run cold. I risked a glance back and saw something large and dark moving through the darkness. Its glowing yellow eyes cut through the shadows like headlights, and its breath came in ragged gasps that made my skin crawl.

"It's gaining on us!" Sara cried.

"We won't outrun it," I said, my mind racing. "We need to slow it down."

"Got an idea?" Riley asked, his voice strained.

"Yeah," I said, yanking the cassette player out of Sara's hands. "We play the tape."

Sara's eyes widened. "Cove, are you crazy? What if it makes things worse?"

"It's a risk we have to take," I said, loading the FINAL MESSAGE tape into the player. My fingers trembled as I pressed PLAY.

The static crackled to life, followed by a slow, haunting 80s synth melody that twisted my stomach. I recognized the song instantly—*Bad Guy* by Billie Eilish—but it wasn't the version I knew and was like the others. The beat dragged behind the melody, and the bass line thumped like a heartbeat underwater. The lyrics were stretched, slurred, and distorted as if they were being sung by someone sinking:

So you're a tough guy... like it really rough guy...
Just can't get enough guy... chest always so puffed guy...

The monster screeched loud, this time as if she was in pain, and then disappeared into the distance, her growls and the smell of lavender disappearing. The warped melody looped, growing louder and more dissonant until it bled into static. Then, Henry Black's voice cut through, desperate and shaking.

"This is my final message. If you're hearing this, you're already in danger. But you need to know the truth. The cargo wasn't what you think."

There was a pause, followed by the sound of him taking a deep, ragged breath.

"We weren't carrying coal or supplies that night. We were carrying death."

I swallowed hard as the weight of his words hit me.

"Thousands of bodies, he continued, his voice cracking. People who had been sacrificed—children, adults, entire families. They were part of some ritual to open a portal to...

something. I don't know what it was, but the bodies were meant to be an offering."

The walls of the tunnel seemed to press in on me, and I could barely breathe.

"But something went wrong. The portal didn't fully open. Instead, it created a tear—something in between. Whatever it was, it attached itself to the train, and by the time we reached the tunnel, it had consumed everything." Henry's voice dropped to a whisper. "I think this has something to do with the hospital…" He pauses again. "The psych hospital, at Halo Hill, I think, I heard suits talking about everything; I don't know what they are up to…" The static returned, and the warped, eerie chorus of *Bad Guy* faded back in cutting him off, the lyrics dragging like they were being sung in slow motion:

I'm that bad type... make your mama sad type... make your girlfriend mad type...

The song dissolved into silence, and the tape clicked off.

I stared at the cassette player, my hands shaking. Henry Black's voice echoed in my head: Thousands of bodies. Sacrifices. The Lavender Lady wasn't just haunting Moonville because of the train accident—she was part of something much darker.

"That's why the monster keeps coming after us," Sara whispered. "It's not just her. It's the ritual."

Stevie wiped the sweat from her brow, her breathing shallow. "Then burning the tapes isn't enough?"

"No," I said, my voice hollow. "We have to find the portal—or whatever's left of it—and destroy it."

Riley groaned. "How the hell are we supposed to do that?"

"We'll figure it out," Sara said, her voice firm. "We have to."

"Wait! The Lavender Lady has been shifting between forms right?" I look around at everyone who looks at me cluelessly.

"Yeah so?" Sara looks at me, annoyed and cautiously looking around her.

"She's been almost glitching the more clues we find, what if she's the portal?"

"That fucking genius!" Stevie says, "The train was a moving portal maybe, and then somehow it got transferred to Emilie Scott that day."

"So, fuck, we have to kill the monster?" Riley takes a deep breath in.

"We have to kill the monster." I repeat.

A loud roar echoed behind us in the far distance, snapping us back to reality. The monster was coming back, and the tunnel walls trembled with each step it took.

"We need to move," I said, pulling Stevie to her feet. "Now!"

We sprinted down the tunnel, the sound of the monster's footsteps closing in behind us. The air grew colder, and the walls dripped with condensation. I could barely see a few feet in front of me, but I kept running, driven by pure adrenaline.

Suddenly, Sara cried out, her foot slipping into a puddle of water. I skidded to a stop and turned back to help her, but my breath caught in my throat.

The puddle wasn't just water. It was moving like the water that attached itself to Stevie earlier.

"Help!" Sara screamed, her leg sinking deeper as the water swirled around her ankle like a living thing.

Riley grabbed her arm and pulled, but the puddle tightened, dragging her down to her knee. "It's fucking alive!" he yelled, panic flashing across his face.

Stevie knelt beside them, grabbing Stevie's other arm. "We've got you!"

I dropped the cassette player and joined them, gripping Stevie's shoulders and pulling with all my strength. The water fought back, churning violently as if it were trying to devour her.

"Don't let go!" Sara cried, tears streaming down her face.

"We won't!" I shouted, gritting my teeth.

The monster's growl echoed through the tunnel, closer now. I could feel its breath on the back of my neck, hot and foul.

"Come on, come on!" Riley grunted, pulling harder.

With one final yank, we tore Sara free, and the puddle collapsed in on itself, splashing harmlessly across the floor. We fell backward, gasping for breath as Sara sobbed in my arms, her leg dripping in blood with multiple gashes as if she got caught in barbed wire.

"Thank you, I'm okay" she whispered, her voice barely audible.

"We're not safe here," Stevie said, picking up the cassette player. "The monster's still coming."

I nodded, my pulse racing. "We need to get out of her like right freaking now!"

We ran through the twisting tunnels, the sound of the monster's footsteps never far behind. My legs burned, and my lungs screamed for air, but I pushed through the pain.

Finally, we emerged into the open air, and I stopped dead in my tracks. The moonlight bathed the tracks in a pale glow, and the scent of lavender was suffocating.

"Riley!" I yell at him in front of me.

"What the fuck are you doing we need to move!" His face and eyes slowly killing me.

"I have an idea, is there a lake, a river, a fucking well, something with water, a lot of water?

"What do you want to go fucking fishing?" He snaps back throwing down his hands.

"The water is alive; it's attacked us twice! Still, calm, harmless water attacked us."

"I hate you! I really, really hate you! Follow me." He starts off running. The girls don't say anything and follow us as we run through the forest away from the city, away from the entrance to Moonville, and deeper into the unknown.

Chapter 14
Revelations of The Curse

The forest breathed around us, the cold, stale air pushing against my skin like icy fingers. We reached a lake that Riley took us to.

"This is not a good place, why would you take us here?" Stevie panted and aggravated.

"He wanted fucking water!" Riley snapped back, catching his breath.

"Why is this place not a good place?" Sara's face tired, her eyeliner dripping from the corner of her eyes.

"This is the area where a lot of people are found dead in Moonville, and this turd brought us here!" She shoves Riley on the shoulder hard as he rubs the sting away.

"This is perfect! We light the tape on fire close to the edge of the water." I look at the three of them. I don't think they even care anymore; at this point, they would do anything.

"The water." Riley stares at me with a smirk.

"The water." I smile back at him. Let's burn these goddamn tapes; she fucking hates it."

We find some dried leaves and sticks, then place the two cassette tapes in the middle, its bold felt tip marker, writing, reading PLAY ME and FINAL MESSAGE, taunting me that this was our life, our beginning, and now our end. Stevie flicks her lighter, sets the leaves on fire, and the flames engulf the plastic. The fire from the burning tapes flickers and casts long shadows on the trees, dancing like ghosts from another time. The scent of lavender was suffocating now, clinging to my hair, clothes, and lungs. The monster's roar echoed from deeper inside the woods, growing louder by the second.

I gripped Sara's hand as we backed away from the pile of burning tapes. Stevie was limping again, but she kept moving, her eyes locked on the flickering flames as if they held the answer to everything.

"Is it working?" Sara asked, her voice trembling.

I didn't know how to answer her. The tapes hissed and crackled, their plastic cases melting and dripping into a black, bubbling pool. Like static electricity, the air around us felt charged just as before lightning strikes. But nothing about this felt like salvation. If anything, it felt like the calm before the storm.

Riley kicked at the fire, scattering bits of smoldering tape across the ground. "This better work, because if it doesn't, we're screwed."

A low, guttural growl echoed through the woods, followed by the sound of something massive scraping against the ground as it snapped the limbs of several trees. The hairs on the back of my neck stood on end, and I tightened my grip on Sara's hand.

"She's coming," Stevie said, her voice barely above a whisper.

We turned toward the sound behind us, and my heart nearly stopped. A figure emerged from the shadows, her form flickering between human and something far more monstrous.

At first, she looked like Emilie Scott—the woman from the ghost tour photos, with her pale skin, dark hair, and piercing eyes. But as she stepped closer, her features twisted and distorted. Her mouth stretched too wide, her teeth sharpened into jagged points, and her eyes glowed like twin lanterns in the dark.

Her dress, once a soft lavender color, now hung in tatters, soaked in blood and dirt. Her arms elongated, the fingers ending in claw-like talons that scraped against the walls as she moved.

"Cove, I'm scared," Sara whispered, her voice trembling as she gripped me tighter.

The realization hit me like a punch to the gut. The Lavender Lady wasn't just a ghost haunting Moonville. She was the curse's living embodiment, a creature born from the failed ritual and the fear of the town's trapped souls.

"Burning the tapes isn't enough," Stevie said, limping back toward us. "We have to destroy her. Cove! Cove!"

The Lavender Lady let out a bone-chilling scream, her voice splitting into multiple pitches like a choir of the dead. The forest floor shook as she ripped a tree limb in anger and threw it above our head it landed in the lake with a splash.

"We have to lure her to get close to the lake," I said, my mind racing.

"And how do you suggest we do that?" Riley asked, his voice dripping with sarcasm. "Ask her nicely?"

"No, I want you to take the girls to the other end of the lake and don't get close to the water." I continue to stare at the beast coming closer to us.

"What!" Riley annoyed and scared.

"Just do it! Go now!" I yell, "Go!"

"Cove!" Sara sobs as Stevie and Riley pry her away from me.

I took a step forward, my heart pounding so hard it felt like it might burst; I heard the water behind me gurgling; I could feel it getting agitated from the tree she threw into the lake. The Lavender Lady's eyes locked onto me, and her lips curled into a cruel smile. Her voice echoed inside my head, soft and venomous.

"You can't save them, Cove. You can't even save yourself."

I swallowed the fear rising in my throat, "You keep saying my name, you ugly bitch, well you have me!"

"Come on," I whisper and take a step backward toward the lake; its splashes haunt whether I will die from this fucking ghost or from mutated monstrous water. "You want me, don't you?" I whisper to myself again."

Her smile widened, revealing rows of sharp teeth. The ground trembled beneath her feet as she took a step toward me.

The Lavender Lady lunged towards me, her claws slashing through the air just inches from my face. I lunged to my right and rolled away from the lake, my breath in ragged gasps. The mutilated beast splashed into the still water like glass shattering; the water agitated, wrapping its tentacles of clear black liquid ink around her. The smell of decay and lavender made my head spin in a petrified horror of sickness. Her horrific cry for help was suffocated by the water as her final breath was overtaken by a monster that even she couldn't escape. I enjoyed watching her die, watching her finally be buried where she couldn't hurt anyone ever again. I watched, not taking a focus off until the water turned into a still, clear black mirror.

"You did it!" Stevie's voice knocked me out of my trance as Sara slammed into me with a hug.

"I think so," I said, my voice shaking.

"Ha, we fucking did it." Riley gives me a push.

We sat there in silence, the weight of what we'd just done pressing down on us. I wanted to believe it was over, that we had broken the curse and could finally leave Moonville. But something inside me wouldn't let go of the doubt.

"We should leave," Riley said, staring at the water.

I nodded, grabbing my backpack. As we walked toward the road, I couldn't help but glance back at the lake one last time. The Lavender Lady was gone, but the memory of her eyes would haunt me forever.

And then, just as we reached the edge of the woods, I saw it—a cassette tape lying in the dirt, its label blank.

My blood turned to ice again, and I thought I'd get used to it by now.

"The curse," I whispered, my throat tightening. "It's not over.

Chapter 15
A Town Reborn

The sun began rising over the distant hills, casting a dull orange glow across the horizon. The warmth should have been comforting, but instead, it only made the emptiness of the forest feel wrong. Too quiet. Too still.

We stood at the edge of the woods, the cassette tape lying between us like a ticking time bomb. My chest tightened as I stared at its blank label, the weight of everything we'd just been through crashing down on me.

"No," Sara said, her voice cracking. "We destroyed the tapes. We burned them. We killed her! How is there another one?"

I knelt down and picked it up, my fingers trembling. The plastic felt warm against my skin as if it had just been created, fresh from whatever force was keeping us trapped here. My mind raced, replaying every moment we'd spent fighting the Lavender Lady, the monster, and the curse. I thought it was over. I wanted it to be over.

"But curses aren't that simple," I said softly.

Riley ran a hand through his hair, his eyes wild. "This can't be happening. We destroyed everything. We literally burned the source, and you, you killed that damn thing!"

Stevie wiped dirt from her face and shook her head. "Maybe... maybe that wasn't the source."

I turned to her, my heart pounding. "What do you mean?"

She gestured toward the woods. "The train crash, the bodies, the portal was just a piece of the curse. But what if the curse isn't tied to one event? What if Moonville itself is the curse?"

Her words hit me like a punch to the gut. The train crash, the Lavender Lady, the monster—they were symptoms, not the cause. The town itself was the disease.

Sara took the tape from my hands, her eyes glistening with tears. "So what do we do now? Burn this one too? Wait for another one to show up?"

I didn't have an answer. My head throbbed, and the smell of smoke and lavender still clung to my clothes, suffocating me. I wanted to scream, to rip the tape apart and throw it into the woods, but I knew it wouldn't change anything. It would just come back like it always did.

"We need to leave," I said, my voice hollow. "Get as far away from Moonville as we can."

"And if the curse follows us?" Stevie asked, her voice barely above a whisper.

"We'll figure it out," I said, the lie burning in my throat. "We have to."

We walked in silence, following the overgrown road that led out of the woods and back toward town. The rising sun painted the trees in shades of gold, but the beauty was lost on me. Every shadow felt like a threat. Every gust of wind carried the memory of the Lavender Lady's whispers.

When we reached the outskirts of town, my stomach twisted. The streets were empty, just like before, but something about them felt... wrong. The houses looked newer, their paint fresh and clean. The cars parked along the sidewalks were in pristine condition, their windows gleaming in the sunlight.

Riley frowned. "Wasn't that car covered in dust before?"

He pointed to a red convertible parked in front of a diner. I remembered seeing it when we first arrived—its windows had been caked with dirt, and its tires flat. Now, it looked like it had just rolled off the lot.

"The town's... fixing itself," Stevie said, her voice trembling. "Like it's resetting."

"Or evolving," Sara added, her hand tightening around mine. "Whatever we did at the lake didn't break the curse. It changed it."

We kept walking, the unease growing with every step. The air was too clean, too crisp as if the town had been scrubbed of its history or was it just a veil. The scent of lavender was gone, replaced by the sterile smell of freshly cut grass and morning dew.

Then, from somewhere in the distance, we heard it.

Music.

We followed the sound, our footsteps quickening as we rounded the corner onto Main Street. The music grew louder, echoing through the empty streets. It was a song I hadn't heard in years, but the haunting familiarity sent chills down my spine.

Running Up That Hill by Kate Bush—but remixed, slowed, and layered with a synth beat that made it sound like a funeral march.

The music led us to the center of town, where a large, glowing screen had been erected in the green grass of the town square. The screen flickered with static before displaying a grainy black-and-white image of a woman standing on the train tracks. Her long, dark hair obscured her face, but I knew who it was.

The Lavender Lady.

"No," Sara whispered, backing away. "We ended this. We ended her."

The woman on the screen lifted her head, her hollow eyes locking onto the camera. Her lips didn't move, but her voice echoed through the speakers, soft and venomous.

"Did you think it would be that easy?"

The screen flickered again, and the image changed. It showed us—me, Sara, Stevie, and Riley—standing in front of the lake again, but this time, it was daylight; it was different. Then, on screen, all four of us turn around and stare upward as if we are looking at ourselves on the other end. My hands were shaking as the image reflected in my eyes like a prophecy of doom and it creeped me the fuck out.

"What the fuck is this?" Riley asked, panic creeping into his voice.

"It's a warning," Stevie said, her face pale. "She's showing us that what we did wasn't enough and that she's watching."

The screen flickered again, and the image zoomed in on all the different cassette tapes that we had burned. But instead of melting into ash, the tapes regenerated, their plastic casing reforming before our eyes one by one.

I felt like I was going to be sick. "It's endless."

The music continued, growing louder and more distorted. The lyrics of *Running Up That Hill* looped, warping until they were unrecognizable:

If only I could make a deal with God... and get him to swap our places...

The song dissolved into static, and the Lavender Lady's voice returned, cutting through the noise like a knife.

"Thank you, Cove."

The screen flickered to the movie *Pretty in Pink*, but the echo of her voice lingered in the air. We stood in silence, the weight of her words sinking in. The town wasn't just resetting—it was expanding its reach. The curse wasn't confined to Moonville anymore. It was evolving, adapting, and preparing to consume everything in its path.

"We have to leave," I said, my voice shaking. "Before it's too late."

Sara grabbed my arm, tears streaming down her face. "And go where? What if we can't outrun it?"

"We have to try," Stevie said, her determination cutting through the fear. "If we stay, we'll become part of it."

Riley nodded. "I'm not dying here, let's try the other side of town."

We turned and ran, our footsteps pounding against the pavement as we headed toward the edge of town. The sun climbed higher, casting long shadows behind us, but I didn't dare look back. The Lavender Lady's voice echoed in my head, and her final warning burned into my memory. The curse is alive. And now, it's spreading.

Epilogue

We crossed the old wooden bridge that marked the town's border, the wind whipping through my hair as we ran. The trees thinned, and for the first time in what felt like forever, I saw the open road stretching out before us.

But even as we reached the highway, a chill settled over me. The air was too still, too quiet. I could still hear the faint echo of Kate Bush's song in my head, like it was following us, waiting for its moment to strike again.

As we walked down the highway, the morning sun casting its warmth over us, I couldn't shake the feeling that the curse was still with us. That it would always be with us. Lurking just beneath the surface, waiting for the right moment to pull us back in, and just as I had the thought, I heard a faint crackle and static coming from the cassette tape that we had found in town from inside my backpack. We didn't get anywhere, we didn't escape. We had walked into the endless loop of this town right back to the entrance of the Moonville tunnel. Trapped here forever.

Look for more books in the
LIMINAL PARADOX series by DAMON ROBI

Damon Robi,

the Dr. Jekyll and Mr. Hyde of writing has been weaving tales of mystery, love, and even a dash of horror since he was a young boy of 13. Born and raised in the Sunshine State, he's a single father of two young boys who still manages to find time to read and write amidst the chaos of parenting.

When he's not busy crafting his next masterpiece, you can find Damon on social media, where he shares snippets of his personal life and the inspirations behind his stories. So, follow Damon on his literary adventures, and who knows? You might just inspire his next great work!

In summary, Damon Robi is a Florida-based author with a penchant for the mysterious and a talent for weaving tales that will leave you spellbound. Follow him on his journey through the written world and beyond.

WWW.DAMON ROBI.COM

Made in the USA
Columbia, SC
07 March 2025

54791569R00079